Open Marriage
A Fatal Attraction Story

I0538299

This is a work of fiction. All of the characters, organizations, and events portrayed in this novel are either products of the author's imagination or are used fictitiously. Any resemblance to actual persons, living or dead, is purely coincidental.

© 2015 Fanita Y. Pendleton Norfolk, VA

Acknowledgments

My son is the light of my life. Helping him grow into a young man has been the single most important thing that I have ever done. I hope him witnessing me fulfill my dreams encourages him to shoot for his. I love you **Brione Lamont Pendleton**.

Family Shout-outs to my: Oakland, California Family; Norfolk, Virginia Family; Oklahoma Family; Texas Family; New York Family; and Hopkinsville, Kentucky Family. Special Shout-out to **Mig** for holding **Urban Moon Productions** down with his debut series, **Dirty Red: A Killa's Love Story**…I love you man. Checkout his work on Nook and Kindle as well as www.Urbanmoonproductions.com.

Shout-out to the **Blaque Diamond Publications** TEAM: Authors Shauntrell Perry, Jauwel, Meka, Roni J, K.L. Hall, Cinnamon Brown, Kieta B, Mimi Ray, Shanard Smith, and Chantel Sills. During the hard times, you guys stood strong. For that, I thank each of you from the bottom of my heart. **Let's Keep Dropping that Heat!!!**

Finally, thank you for being a part of my movement. A special shout-out goes to all the authors and readers who support me by downloading, reading, and reviewing my work.

Follow me on *Twitter:* @Moon081471

Instagram: Fanita Pendleton

Connect with me on *Facebook*: Fanita Moon Pendleton

Website: www.Urbanmoonproductions.com

Join my Readers Group on *Facebook*: Fanita Moon Pendleton's Readers

Please be sure to leave your review. Reviews are important to authors. Not only do they give you a voice, they are also important to potential readers who want to hear from someone who has read the book and how they liked it. I appreciate your support…

Moon

Open Marriage A Fatal Attraction Story

By

Fanita Moon Pendleton

Another Wild Ass Weekend

The smell of bacon lingered in the air as Jason completed the breakfast he planned to serve his wife in bed. He gave himself a pound as he placed the pancakes, bacon, scrambled eggs, strawberries, and orange juice on a serving tray. After the performance his woman put down last night, he figured the least he could do was spoil her this morning.

Most women would kill to have a man like Jason, he knew it too. He was tall–well over six feet; he played football in college, and even in his thirties, still had the workout habits of an athlete. His momma used to tell him women were gonna eat him up. The thought made him smile because as a kid, he had no idea what she meant. When he turned thirteen, he gave them the chance to eat his dick every chance he got.

Jason was from a stable, two-parent family with a father who was the president of a franchise bank and a mother who was the dean at a state college. He had an older brother, Tony, and younger sister, Sheila, who were both successful in their own rights.

All of the Matthews children were brought up to respect the Matthews name, period. In his mind, he was the total package.

He had a seven figure salary, was what women called drop-dead fine, knew his dick game was on point, and he wasn't afraid of commitment.

Women threw themselves all over Jason, but he was good on that once he met Bri. The moment he saw her, she sucked the air right out of his lungs without even trying. Like all the other women, she didn't throw herself at him and he liked that. Jason wasn't used to a woman who was sexy beyond measure but wasn't stuck on herself. She had her own career, own house, no kids, and was a free spirit. It wasn't like him to fall for a woman; hell, women usually tripped over him, but with Bri it was different. Scooping up the tray, he began to make his way to the bedroom with his male organ swinging from thigh to thigh. The food was smelling good, the tray looked scrumptious, and he felt like a playboy.

His room was beyond elegant, from its lush gold and purple colors to its over-sized sitting room. It was definitely a relaxing retreat.

The lights were dim and the smooth sounds of the Isley Brothers, "Between the Sheets" was on repeat. But the centerpiece and Jason's pride and joy would have to be his Prado California King bed.

It wasn't just the intricate carvings and moldings, or the footboard that was curved to match the oversized headboard design; it was all the sexual relief that took place in his bed on a daily basis. It was by far the most used area in the room. Jason approached the bed, balancing the tray; he couldn't help but smile internally at how blessed he was. He had the baddest chick in the game and there was no doubt about that. The pride he had because of it was beyond measure. Standing over the bed, he stared down at her round ass, admiring the firmness of it.

6

He had always been an ass man, but the thickness of Bri's thighs peeking through the silk sheets threatened to change his mind.

Before he could wake her, there was movement in the sheets. The legs he had just been admiring suddenly doubled and Candi stuck her head up with a smile. Jason smiled back at his wife's playmate. She was sexy as hell and almost as thick as Bri with a creamy skin tone.

This was not Candi's first time in his bed; her lustful sexiness caused his dick to salute her like an obedient soldier as his mind drifted to the activities of the previous night.

Jason licked the lining out of a pussy so sweet that juices trickled down the sides of his mouth. He attacked her as if he hadn't eaten for days. Candi tasted exactly like her name implied and Jason was trying to taste every inch of her.

Not to be outdone, Bri mounted his thickness, allowing Jason to sink balls deep in her pleasure palace. Both Candi and Bri enjoyed their ride as they became entangled in a kiss that heightened their pleasure. The smell in the air was sweet and sticky, just like he liked it. Pound for pound, Jason put in work, giving each lady exactly what they needed.

He could feel himself nearing his own climax. Once Bri really put that vice grip pussy on him and started moving at a faster pace, he knew she was almost ready herself. The moans in the room appeared to get louder as Candi screamed out her release first. Her entire body began to shake uncontrollably.

The sensation from her movement caused a ripple effect. Bri's juices could be heard swooshing around as she made her final descent into ecstasy as she screamed, "Shiiiiiiiiiiiiiiiiiiiiiiiid, I'm commmmming!"

That's all Jason needed to hear as he gripped her waist then slammed his dick as far as it would go all the way through her Orgasm. Right before Bri finished her climb to the top of the rollercoaster, Jason exploded, causing her to begin shaking all over again. "Yes baby...come on daddy's dick...urrrrg fuckkkkkk!"

It always turned Bri on when Jason released his seed, no matter what state of sexual bliss she was in, she would come all over again.

The sensation of his dick swimming in wetness broke his trance. At first, he thought he was still daydreaming, but he opened his eyes to find Candi slurping every inch of his meat. For a second, he thought about stopping her to prevent the intense pleasure she was giving him. He really wasn't into playing around if Bri wasn't involved. Instead, he gave in and closed his eyes as he savored the feeling while attempting to not drop the tray.

The loud slurping must have awakened Bri, because when Jason opened his eyes again, he was greeted with the sexy smile of his woman. He loved his woman so much; she was everything he needed.

Bri gave him a sexy wink and said, "Thank you for bringing us breakfast baby," then immediately joined Candi as they both shared him for their morning meal.

Jason felt his knees getting weak but there was nowhere for him to put the tray. The pleasure he was receiving from both women was too much to handle.

One was deep-throating him with a mouth like a fast moving waterfall. The other had his balls down her throat, causing him to feel tingling from his toes to the top of his ears. Jason couldn't hold back any longer. He yelled his release, overshadowing the music playing in the room as well as the crashing breakfast tray that he dropped.

Bri

Glamour Girls, Inc. was the largest makeup distributor of African American beauty products in the world. Briann Jennings was the CEO and the brains behind every aspect of the business. Her best friend, Marta VanDyke, was a strong, sexy, white girl that Bri went to college with; she was her right-hand man. Together, they had made the Fortune 500 Top Business of the year for the fifth year running. With offices in the largest building in downtown Norfolk, Bri made sure her company maintained its image.

Slightly leaning back in her Herman Miller Embody Chair, Bri stared out the window of her penthouse suite with her ink pen in her mouth, a nasty habit she did when she was in deep thought. Her mind was drifting over her life, accomplishments, and her marriage. Thinking about Jason always brought a smile to her eyes, but today it caused anxiety. They had been married for two years now and although Jason was everything she needed, Bri was beginning to think he wasn't everything she wanted. Jason was on board with her alternative lifestyle.

It was the one stipulation she had when he asked her to marry him.

She informed him in no uncertain terms that she wanted an open marriage. Like any man, Jason thought he had hit the lottery and was down for it. However, he had stipulations of his own. They both had to agree on the partner and no one could party without the other.

It seemed like an easy compromise, but right now, as she sat looking into the sky, Bri wondered if she could keep up her end of the bargain. Bri let her mind wander back to when she was still single and Jason walked into her life, sweeping her off her feet and knocking her off her game.

The Brinks Lounge was always packed. However, the party didn't really start until Bri and her girls walked in. They commanded attention from the valet to the dance floor. Sexy was an understatement, these women had their own money and turned down thirsty niggas on a regular. The music was live and the beautiful people were in the house. Bri and her girls, Shonda and Reann, were chillin in VIP, laughing loudly and enjoying each other's company.

Shonda ran her family's Magnus Hotel in Vegas; she was only in town once a month. Reann was a criminal defense attorney with her own booming firm.

They were all single, no kids, gainfully employed, and fly as hell. They were the quintessential IT girls! They had a standing date once a month to party like rock stars and let their hair down. They rarely missed the opportunity to do just that.

"Girl, that's my jam right there!" Reann exclaimed, jumping up from the white couch, swaying her thick hips from side-to-side.

"Good Kisser" blared from the speaker. Glancing around the club, Reann had her eye on some fellas that looked like they fit the bill.

She turned to the ladies and waved saying, "Ok ladies, 'bout to go out here and find out what's really going on; I came here to party. Whoo! Whoo!" She pumped her fist and sauntered her size 18 thickness dressed to kill into the crowd, grabbing hold of a dude wearing Armani, not that handsome but definitely swagging it out.

Bri could do nothing but laugh; she knew exactly how her girls were. When they got together, it was all about sisterhood and having a good time. Looking at Shonda,

Bri gave her the eye saying, "Girl, I'm 'bout to get like Re and get my groove on. Momma feeling a little frisky tonight, so I might be choosing." Both ladies burst out laughing, got up, and left VIP to have some fun.

One thing about The Brinks Lounge was its upscale appeal, from the VIP treatment throughout the lounge to the relaxing atmosphere. It was definitely the place to be in the Norfolk area. The patrons were the movers and shakers of the city looking for a place to mingle and let their hair down. That's exactly what they were able to do at The Brinks Lounge, which was members only. If you weren't a member, it cost $250 at the door, this increased the feeling of exclusivity.

Bri was dressed in fitted tuxedo pants with black red bottoms. Her white halter showed off her ample chest and flat stomach. Her look was flawless; the attention she garnered as she strolled through the crowd was a testament to her appeal.

She spotted Romello, CEO of Mello Music, but continued to walk as if she didn't see him. Romello was the type of dude women chased and Bri was not a chaser; she didn't have to be. Besides, for the last six months, Romello had been on her phone daily, trying to get to the center of the Tootsie Roll pop.

Bri planned on giving him some, just to see what all the fuss was about, but she still wanted to make sure he knew he didn't run a damn thang when it came to Briann Jennings.

Mello pushed up on Bri and whispered in her ear, "So what a brotha gotta do to get next to a beautiful woman like you?"

Without showing it on her face, Bri smiled. She knew exactly who was behind her; she could feel his appreciation pressed up against her ass.

"Humm, you can dance with me Mello." Bri looked over her shoulder and gave her award winning smile before she headed to the crowded dance floor. She was sure to make her ass move in a way to hypnotize anyone watching.

The music slowed down then KEM blared from the speakers. "Love Calls" was one of Bri's favorite jams. Not because she wanted to be in love, hell, she wasn't even sure she believed in love in it's purest form. What she really did love was the way KEM made it sound. Romello pulled her closer; her head hit him dead center in his chest.

He smelled like Eternity, which brought a smile to her face as she thought to herself; there ain't nothing like a good smelling man. The slow grind they were doing was so erotic damn near everyone stopped to watch. They were making love in the club, and many onlookers were hating hard for different reasons. The women wanted Mello, he was a Boss. Bri had her own admirers, male and female. Although she was single, she turned people down daily like she was snatched up. On this day, one of her admirers was Jason.

The music changed to a hot new joint that was playing daily in heavy rotation on the radio. The crowd went crazy. Romello did his best Shamoney dance while Bri showed him how she made it twerk. She felt a tingle in her spine; it was the same tingle she felt every time he was near.

Bri knew he was somewhere close, watching her. When she looked up mid twerk, she locked eyes with Jason. She knew exactly who Jason Matthews was.

He was one of the youngest owners of a Fortune 500 company, JM Advertising. They always ran into each other at black tie functions. His company even produced several commercials for Glamour Girls. Whenever he was near her, she felt even sexier than she already was. There was something about him that she couldn't put her finger on. Just because he was watching, Bri began to give her twerk a little extra juice. They never broke the trance they were under; they simply talked to each other through their eyes. They had a full-fledged conversation without once opening their mouths.

Bri thought she heard Jason ask her what she was doing with that nigga. Well that's what she thought she heard and it made her giggle.

The song ended and Bri was ready to catch up with her girls. She gave Mello a quick hug who attempted to hold on just a little too long as he said, "So that's all a nigga get from you Bri? Why you keep playing me?" Mello wore a hurt expression as he talked close to her face.

Bri couldn't believe Mello was acting like that. He was letting his street hang all the way out. "Mello, you already know me and you don't rock like that. Come to me when you get out ya feelings then we might have something to talk about." Bri left Mello in the middle of the dance floor, watching her ass sway from side-to-side.

Years ago, Bri decided she didn't want to fuck with a nigga who was gonna be trying to wife her and put demands and labels on her. She would decide when and if that happened and planned on being in total control of her own destiny as well as her pussy. When she made it back to VIP, neither of her girls were there, which was just fine. Bri sat down on the plush, white, leather sofa and poured herself a glass of Moet then allowed the atmosphere to take her away.

Her groove was interrupted by her favorite waitress, Danielle. At 5'2", she was a sassy beauty that patrons loved to see coming. She was the type of waitress that guaranteed your evening out with your girls was an experience.

Exclusively working VIP meant you never had to wait for anything when she was in control of the area. She walked into the booth carrying a slender glass and bottle in a gold bucket.

"Hey Bri, girl who is this nigga cashing out on you? This that Italian Pinot Grigio, girl. This that good stuff." With a sexy smile, Danielle poured Bri half a glass of the expensive wine.

Bri giggled as she watched her pour one of the best tasting wines she had ever had. Her mind was wandering because not too many people knew about her love of wines, especially the good ones. Pinot Grigio happened to be one of her absolute favorites, due to its light and fruity taste. Bri knew damn well Romello didn't take the time to learn that much about her. All he wanted was some ass, something like this was from a man who wanted more.

Sipping the wine, she smiled as she inhaled the fragrance of Issey Miyake. "I guess I have you to thank for the Pinot?" Bri turned to face the figure that was looming at the VIP entrance. Jason cracked a smile displaying the sexiest smile she had ever seen on a man. It wasn't just that he was pleasing to the eye, his eyes held a genuineness that was hard to fake.

"I thought it was time that we met formally, don't you?" He said in a voice so deep you would have thought Barry White was standing in the room. Jason had that Idris Elba walk, the kind that assured you he was packing a monster.

Bri had to shake her head as she watched him come closer; she had never really experienced the vibe she was feeling with him being so near. She heard girlfriends talk about a dude making them feel giddy, but Bri had always been immune. She made niggas and bitches giddy, got her rocks off then carried her ass. But for some reason, Jason intrigued her.

"You are absolutely right. No black tie, no work, but in our natural habitat without any inhibitions." She replied as she patted the couch beside her for him to have a seat.

After that night, they were inseparable, well as inseparable as their demanding careers permitted. Bri learned to allow someone into her world without fear of rejection or betrayal. The chime on her computer indicated that she had a new email. She had to stop daydreaming and focus on the here and now. Turning her attention to her computer, she clicked on an email from an unknown sender. Instantly, she rolled her eyes. Lately, Bri had been getting a lot of unknown sender emails.

I don't know what they think they're accomplishing by sending me this shit, she thought. Reading the latest email she had a slight smirk.

Jason is a good man and deserves better than a bitch like you!

The message was always the same; and of course, it wasn't signed. Shaking her head, Bri closed out of her email, thinking to herself, *Ain't nobody got time for that shit.*

Whoever thinks they got what it takes to take Jason from a BITCH like me is welcomed to try. I am unbothered, because I am 'That Bitch' believe that!

There was a knock on her door and the email was quickly forgotten. Clearing her throat, she said, "Come in." The thick, mahogany door opened and in walked Charmaine, her wizard of an assistant. Wearing an inquisitive expression on her face, she moved quickly toward her boss's desk.

"Ms. Bri, I buzzed your line but didn't get an answer." Charmaine stated as she stood center mass in front of Bri's heirloom desk.

Bri was admiring her choice in outfits today–a burnt orange and navy pencil skirt with a cream blouse as she asked, "Who are you wearing today, Charmaine? I like it on you."

The smile that came from Charmaine lit up the entire room as she answered, "This is from Marc Jacobs' new line. I absolutely love it. I really appreciate you giving all of us a clothing budget. The whole office looks like new money." Charmaine gushed as she snapped her fingers.

Bri chuckled; she had made the decision that with the New Year her staff needed to look the part of a Fortune 500 team. Therefore, she set up accounts with all of the top designers. Each employee had an account and a monthly stipend. All Bri asked in return was that they always look their best.

Nodding her head she replied, "All of you are representing Glamour Girls well and you are very welcome. I'm sorry; I was working and didn't hear you. What do you need?"

Holding up her notepad, Charmaine looked at the name she had written and said, "There is a Hudson Duke here to see you.

He doesn't have an appointment but I know he is a heavy hitter, so I wanted to check with you to see if you had time to meet with him."

Bri's panties got moist at the mention of Duke, that's what everyone called him, no one called him Hudson. In the past, Bri had several run-ins with him and had been wanting to have a face-to-face with him for years, but she always played it cool. After all, Duke was the competition. He was next in line at BM-Beauty Mark, Inc. Unlike Bri, Duke was raised in money. He was the only child of wealthy parents who built their company from the ground up. BM always had a strong hold on the mainstream cosmetic market. Momma Duke was a former fashion model turned mogul, who defied the industry, not only by being a top business woman, but challenging the prejudices of the world by marrying a black man. She capitalized on her knowledge of the industry and beauty products. Her company cornered the popular beauty market. When she met Poppa Duke, he was a big time executive in Paris and he swept her off her feet. It was Poppa Duke's idea to delve into the black beauty market.

Beauty Mark, Inc. held the majority of the black market's dollar until Bri's Glamour Girls showed up on the scene.

His mother was head of the company on paper only. Duke had been running the show for over five years. Five years ago, two tragedies happened right behind each other, Poppa duke died, and Momma Duke had a massive stroke. They were still a valuable company but were destined to remain behind Glamour Girls in the consumer market as well as product distribution and celebrity endorsements. Even white consumers were sliding away from them as more and more makeup artists began to see the value in utilizing African American cosmetics to enhance their features. Duke was irresistible in appearance but that wasn't what attracted Bri, it was his confidence. Furthermore, he was a man's man, which made Bri weak. It was killing her to know why he was in her office.

Looking up from her computer, Bri attempted to act as though she was unbothered as she said, "Charmaine, send him in. And oh, hold all my calls."

Charmaine nodded her head then turned to go back to her office with a knowing look on her face. *I don't know who Bri thinks she's fooling, she wanna fuck that man.*

But that's good for me, because I wanna fuck Jason, so this might work in my favor. Just as she finished her thought, she was back in her office. Giggling to herself the entire time, she ushered Duke toward Bri's waiting arms.

Marta

The buzzing of the Turbo Bullet was humming lightly as Marta allowed it to settle over her dripping clit. The electric sensations were causing the leg that was propped on her desk to shiver as the bullet took total control of her senses. She moaned loudly as she neared her peak with only one person on her mind, Bri. Marta was so turned on by her friend that she often snuck away when she was at work just to relieve the sexual tension. The main problem for Marta was that she was completely heterosexual and had never even had a sexual thought about another woman. Yet, Bri managed to make Marta feel like she was missing something by not being more adventurous.

The women met in college and struck up a friendship but didn't run in the same circles. It wasn't until their junior year that things changed for them. They both realized they were the first to arrive and the last to leave when it came to any business related classes or functions. Based on that, they began talking about their interests and the type of business they wanted to own one day.

When Bri told Marta about her idea for a black beauty product empire, Marta was really impressed with the thought she had put into it. She knew the current market landscape, demographics, and products to gear them toward. Bri truly understood her target audience and how best to serve them. Marta knew she could bring marketing expertise to the table of any business and proposed to Bri that they work on her business plan together. They began spending all of their free time together, planning the takeover of the beauty world.

One night, Marta spent the night at Bri's dorm after one of their late night pow wows and was awakened by the sound of Bri moaning loudly. Marta didn't want her to know she was awake, so she was sure to be very quiet as she positioned herself to see what all the commotion was about. What she saw changed the way she looked at sex and intrigued her at the same time. Bri was stretched out on the couch in the dorm room. However, Marta couldn't see her face because there was an extremely beautiful black woman sitting on her face. She was grinding her pussy into Bri's face, moaning loudly. Actually, she was the loud voice that Marta heard.

Bri's legs were spread eagle with a well-stacked lady between them sucking on her pussy. Marta found herself panting as she moved her hands between her legs and began to twirl her fingers around her own clit. She couldn't believe she was dripping like she was from watching women have sex. The shaking of her leg was a sure sign that she was nearing her climax. Just as she heard screaming from the sexcapade across the room, she yelled out her release. Marta was sweating and having aftershocks; she couldn't remember the last time she'd cum that hard.

Her legs were shaking uncontrollably as she opened her eyes and yelled out her release. Thinking about that night in the college dorm always made her cum quick and hard. After that day, she never looked at Bri the same. For the last ten years, she had been silently admiring her from afar. Marta was so pissed when Bri got married. Buried deep in the back of her mind, she believed Bri belonged to her. Although sexy in her own right, Marta never married and rarely dated. She was thinking it was time to make a move to tell Bri how she felt.

Duke

There was a large amount of activity going on around Glamour Girls, Inc. Duke was impressed with the class and elegance of the offices and office staff. There were well-placed pictures of movie stars mounted on the walls. All of whom utilized Glamour Girls' products. There was a huge picture of Kishara, the current face of Glamour Girls. She was breathtaking and represented the Glamour Girls brand well. Duke had been watching Briann Jennings for years. At one time, he thought about pursuing her romantically but then she up and got married. Married women were off-limits to him. It was a Duke rule that he tried very hard to honor. He had witnessed firsthand the hurt and pain that infidelity caused when his father's second family was revealed, so he tried to stay far away from it. But he couldn't lie and say he wasn't extremely attracted to Bri, and it always took every bit of restraint he had not to say fuck his self-imposed rules. Despite all of that, today was about business, so he would have to put all of those thoughts behind him.

Tapping on the door, he heard a sexy voice tell him to come in. The office was no less luxurious than the rest of the building. Duke stopped for a minute and just stared. There she was in all her glory, the Queen of Beauty as she was called in the media. Walking toward her desk in his self-assured manner, he flashed his dazzling white smile. With his 6'3" frame, milk chocolate skin tone, and solid body, most women fell to their knees whenever he came on the scene, but not Bri and Duke liked that. Taking a seat in one of the plush wing chairs, he broke the silence.

"It's been a long time Bri, but I see you're doing well." His smile was dazzling and he knew it.

The deep baritone in his voice did not help Bri as she tried to control the wetness between her legs. Crossing her legs behind her desk and with a sassy smile, he reply was, "Well if it's not the Duke of Beauty! What brings you to my neck of the woods?" Her question belied how she was really feeling. The strong laugh caught her off-guard but excited her as well.

"I know you're a busy woman Bri, but I wanted to come by personally and discuss a business proposition with you from a Duke to a Queen." He crossed his legs then leaned back in his seat.

Hearing the word business brought Bri out of her sexual fog. She uncrossed her legs and sat up in her seat. Noticing the change, Duke realized he had her undivided attention now. If nothing else, Bri was known to be a shrewd business woman. Even though he could tell she was feeling him right now, he knew there was no way she would allow that to interfere with business. He watched with a sly smile as Bri leaned forward and asked, "How may I help you, Duke?"

Jason

Jason was having a relaxing lunch with his best friend, Brent. They went to college together and both went into the business field. Jason was the owner of JM Advertising. He handled the commercial traffic for all the major networks. Brent, on the other hand, created commercials for all the major networks. Therefore, when they got together, they always had plenty to talk about. However, Brent always wanted to know what kind of kinky shit Jason had been into lately. Brent had finally gotten married a year and a half after Jason and now had triplets at home. Thus, he lived his life vicariously through Jason and his adventures. When Jason first told him about the open arrangement in his marriage, Brent told him he was the luckiest man alive. As he sipped his juice, Jason questioned if that was true.

"Check it out Brent, I ain't gon' lie, being able to fuck different women and watch my wife fuck them is the biggest turn on in the world. Watching another nigga fuck my wife though, is something that still doesn't sit too well with me."

Brent was nodding his head up and down as he chewed and tried to speak at the same time. "Yeah Jay, I damn sure wouldn't be able to watch another nigga fuck my Queen." He had a look of disgust on his face that brought the situation home.

Jason put a fry in his mouth as he stared at his friend. "See, so the shit ain't all peaches and cream like you thought." Jason's fingers were pointing back and forth between himself and Brent as he continued.

"As men, we don't mind another chick in the bed, but you don't wanna run a train on your wife with no ashy ass nigga." Chewing his fry, he was starting to feel a little ill as what he said hit home. Jason loved the life he had with Bri and definitely enjoyed the perks, but he was thinking it was time for him and Bri to settle down, have some kids, and close the open door to their marriage. The only problem was he didn't know how to break the news to Bri. It was funny because if you would have asked him years ago if he would turn down a wife who wanted to have threesomes, he thought he would've never wanted to put an end to that action.

Brent cleared his throat to get Jason's attention. He could tell the conversation kind of had his buddy in his feelings. "Ok Jason, I see where you're coming from. Everything that glitters ain't gold. Honestly, I'm really not that much into sharing for real. I guess the question is, what are you gonna do from here?" Brent raised one eyebrow as he asked the question, causing his forehead to wrinkle.

Jason put his drink down and sat back in his chair. His shoulders dropped and his face registered that he didn't know what to do. "I don't know Brent; I know Bri and she wants what she wants. Hell, this was all her idea, so I doubt she's gonna like the fact that I wanna change the game in the 9th inning. I guess my hope is that she loves me and values our marriage enough to walk away from that lifestyle." Having lost his appetite, Jason pushed back from the table, looking a little loss. Just this weekend, he was fucking the shit out of Bri's friend, Candi, and now he wants to have a strictly monogamous relationship with his wife.

The reality is he was tired of sharing his lady, plain and simple, that's what it came down to. Therefore, he was about to put his foot down. He was so deep in thought that he didn't hear his cell phone buzzing and vibrating the table.

The buzzing didn't go unnoticed by Brent who clapped his hands loudly to get Jason's attention. "Jay! Damn man, this shit got you shook, you don't even hear your phone." He shook his head as Jason snapped back to reality then picked up his phone with a sheepish grin.

"My bad, I do have a lot on my mind though." Jason said as he touched the message icon on his phone. He didn't recognize the number but he recognized the message as he read it. It was the same message he had been getting for weeks. *Your Wife is not the woman you think she is, you deserve better.* Slamming the phone down on the table, Jason received stares from people at other tables but he didn't care. He was pissed that someone was playing games with his relationship. Looking at his boy, he simply said, "Bitches play too much!"

Already knowing what it was, Brent looked up from his desert and shrugged his shoulders. "Who was that, The Phantom?" It was the name they had given the mystery person sending the elusive texts. Before Jason could answer, Brent said, "Same shit, different day?

Pulling his money from his wallet, Jason was clearly not happy. "Yeah B, chicks be on that bullshit, but they can't stop what Bri and I have so fuck it.

This is one of the reasons why I wanna get people out of our personal life, because there's no telling which one of these freak bitches is playing on my damn phone. You give them some good dick, supposedly on that no strings shit, and everybody wants to be a puppet. I'm sick of it really."

Lunch was over and Jason was more determined than ever to convince Bri. He made up his mind that tonight would be the night to put it all on the table.

Marta

The light buzzing from the Turbo Bullet made a sensual sound throughout the office. Marta's legs were shaking slightly and juices were leaking to the plush carpet as she let the bullet roam around her clit. She was no stranger to bringing herself to climax and being around Bri was all the motivation she needed. Sometimes, she would dip into her office two or three times a day to release her pent-up frustration. Marta was not attracted to women and had never experienced sex with a woman, but there was something about Bri that always made her weak in the knees.

Marta's body was shaking so hard that it snapped her out of her trance. She yelled out her release as the bullet fell to the floor. Anytime she thought about that night in the dorm, it sent her senses into overdrive. Still feeling slight aftershocks, Marta tried to regain her composure. She had been carrying this torch for Bri for ten years. Although she was a dime piece in her own right, she rarely dated. To satisfy her needs, she had a couple of friends that she connected with, but she made sure she didn't engage in any committed relationships.

She put her all into the business and watching Bri from afar. Marta had finally built up enough courage to at least tell Bri how she was feeling. Sadly, the moment was ruined the day that Bri announced she was marrying Jason. That's when everything changed.

The ringing of the private office line sobered her up real quick. Sitting up straight in her chair, she fixed her skirt, blushing at the realization of what had just occurred. Perking up, she quickly grabbed the phone. "Hey Bri, what's up!"

Bri sensed something funny in Marta's voice. Then again, Marta always sounded funny so she overlooked it. "Marta, you will never believe what Duke wanted when he came to see me today."

Marta cringed when she heard Duke had been in the office. She knew Bri had the hots for Duke and didn't want another person in the way; she already had Jason to deal with. Her entire demeanor changed as she said, "What did that vulture want? You know we have to watch ourselves around him; he just wants our secrets." Marta hoped throwing salt in the game would make Bri see her logic.

Bri chuckled slightly because she knew Marta had a little crush on her but she wasn't entertaining it. Marta was her girl and a wiz with the numbers. However, despite Bri's lifestyle, she had never been attracted to her. Bri was sure it was because she was white but didn't really want to put it on that. She made the decision that their friendship wasn't worth it. Still laughing, she told Marta to meet her in the conference room so they could discuss Duke's proposal.

Charmaine

It had been a long day in the Glamour Girls camp and Charmaine for one was ready for it to end. Looking out the window from her office in the penthouse, she could see the afternoon sun setting and the evening glow making its appearance. She smiled slightly at her luck in securing a job working for the boss; she envied Bri. Her forehead wrinkled as the reality of that thought entered her head. Standing quickly, she pouted out loud to an empty room…*She's perfect and gets everything she wants, even Jason!* The jealously she felt toward Bri was overwhelming her. It wasn't like Charmaine wasn't a good-looking woman in her own right; she was stacked with beautiful features. Men hit on her all the time. Unfortunately, none of her relationships went anywhere. In fact, the last two didn't end well. There were incidents of abuse, cursing, stalking, and destruction of property, all caused by Charmaine.

Most men thought she was obsessive and clingy. When they attempted to end the relationship, Charmaine would lose her mind. Her last boyfriend, Ron, had her arrested when she set his clothes on fire in his bathtub.

The fire spread to the entire bathroom before it could be contained by the fire department. The shit was serious; someone could have died, but just like when she got into trouble in the past, her Uncle Presley, who was a big wig in city government, intervened and she was never formally charged. She did have to pay a settlement to Ron for damages and agree not to come within 500 feet of him. If Charmaine breached the agreement, there wouldn't be anything Uncle Presley could do for her.

All of this happened a little over two years ago, right about the time that Bri and Jason got married. It was a low point for Charmaine, she felt lonely. When Bri brought her new husband to a company dinner, Charmaine was immediately smitten with the handsome man on her arm. Like everything else that Bri had, Charmaine wanted Jason for herself and had every intention of getting him.

Shutting down her computer, Charmaine prepared to leave for the day as she continued to hold onto her fantasy. She was making plans to make Jason her man and didn't care who got mad about it.

Bri needs to just move on 'cause Jason doesn't really want her nasty ass anyway. I see how he looks at me when he comes to this office. He needs a real woman. I hate when bitches can't buy a clue, she thought.

Judgment Night

Jason made it home early from a long day of trying to balance working on new accounts with soul searching. He couldn't take anymore, so he called it quits three hours earlier than usual. The shit going on in his personal life had taxed his brain all damn day. People assumed he had it all together because he was handsome, made good money, and was happily married. They had no clue about all the shit that went on in his head on a daily basis, thinking to himself, *The grass is not always greener.* Usually, the drive home from a long day helped clear his head, but not today. He was still fucked up about the latest text message from the Phantom. Talking louder than the old school rap that was lightly playing from his Bose speakers. "What the fuck is the point? Bri is my wife for better or worse. I can't even imagine why this person thinks they can come between that." He expressed all of the thoughts that were swirling through his head as he pulled into his massive driveway. Jason planned to shut out the outside noise, refusing to let it interfere with his plans. He made up his mind that tonight was the night he would have a serious talk with Bri and the outside world was not invited.

Walking through his massive mansion, one would think a rock star or movie star lived there. It was definitely decked out. From the high ceilings to the grand foyer, he knew his home was the shit. Jason gave all the credit for décor of the crib to Bri and her impeccable taste. Stepping into his larger than life chef's kitchen, he placed his bags on nothing but the best granite.

His plan of attack was to bring on the romance, Bri loved that shit. Chuckling to himself, Jason admitted that he liked to do these kind of things for Bri just to see her smile. That's how a nigga knows he's met his soul mate when he's rushing home from work to cook her dinner. Nothing could take the smile from his face as he picked up the remote control and clicked the button that turned on the surround sound. As Babyface's melodic voice started to float through his home, Jason set out to prepare Bri her favorite meal. He had to admit, his kitchen skills were off the chain. Most women didn't even know how to act when a man knew his way around the kitchen. He also planned to open up the rarely used elegant dining room and switch the music selection to smooth jazz, which was her favorite. Looking around carefully, he wanted to make sure he wasn't missing anything; he wanted everything to be perfect when Bri arrived home.

With the action in the kitchen under control, Jason made his way to the dining room to set the mood. The elegance in the formal dining room couldn't be outdone, but as he stood near the mahogany wood Chippendale table with seating for twelve, Jason realized he wanted something more intimate. As if a light bulb went off in his head, Jason began rearranging his initial idea. Most men didn't understand what he was going through right now, not even Brent. Hell, some men might even think he was on some bitch shit. More than likely, they'd never really had someone who represented everything they wanted in a woman. Most of Jason's friends were too busy chasing behind bitches, hoping that one day they would run into that rare jewel, but never believing it would actually happen.

Jason knew who that man was; hell he used to be that man. Before he met Bri, he was on a never-ending spiral of one-night stands, booty calls, and hookups. In fact, he actually got to the point where he and his boys expected it to be that way forever.

They were running around just like the boys in the movie *The Wood* with the attitude that they would hang out together for the rest of their lives. Getting older, Jason started looking at shit differently.

Was there really life after the club, was a question that he and all of his friends had to answer for themselves. Thankfully, Bri saved him from that reality. After dating her for six months, he popped the question. Luckily, Bri said yes, well with her own set of stipulations, but she said yes nonetheless. Two years later, he knew he'd made the best decision of his life.

Two hours later, the tantalizing smells of seafood gumbo, Bri's favorite, was making it hard to concentrate, but he still had a lot of work to do to pull off the perfect romantic evening. The nights were in that awkward space between summer and fall. With the temperature being between 65 to 70 degrees in the evening, Jason decided he would take advantage of that for dinner. With his time winding down before Bri sashayed through the front door, he went to the bedroom and sprinkled rose petals on the floor, placed something sexy on the bed then went into the bathroom to prepare a bath in the 72 inch, cast iron, claw foot bathtub.

He would wait until he saw her Mercedes pull into the driveway before he actually started the bath; he wanted the water to be nice and hot just like she liked it. Jason was pulling out all the stops. He felt like he would get some pullback from Bri, but he wanted to be able to show her that making a change in their marital lifestyle wouldn't be all bad. Jumping in the shower, he was thinking about what he would say to Bri to get her onboard.

Change

Thirty minutes later, Bri entered her elegant foyer after a long day at the office. She had some serious business decisions to make, but decided to leave that stress at the door. The continued emails were also long forgotten. All she wanted to do was cuddle up with her husband and relax. A smile immediately creased her lips as her senses were tickled with the aromas lingering in the air. Placing her briefcase on a foyer chair, she moved effortlessly through her home, following her nose to the kitchen. She knew exactly what she smelled; it was her favorite. From past experiences, she knew if Jason was cooking seafood gumbo, he was trying to bribe her into doing something or someone. With that last sexy thought, her mind began to wander about who could possibly be joining them. Shaking her head as she stood over the large stewpot, Bri allowed the aroma to invade her nostrils while her mind thought about another part of her body that needed to be filled up.

Making her way up the spiral staircase, Bri had butterflies in her stomach. She had to admit that her man really set the mood with the smells and sounds he'd created.

The surround sound followed her down the hallway as the smooth sounds of The Teddy Bear, Gerald Levert's, "Deep As It Goes" made its contribution to the sexy atmosphere. As soon as she pushed the double doors to her master suite open, her eyes lit up like it was Christmas. From the door entry all the way to the bed, there were red rose petals on the plush, cream carpet.

The contrast between the two colors took Bri's breath away as she strolled around her large room looking from side-to-side as if she expected someone to jump out and say surprise. When she turned toward her massive bed and saw the sparkles against her black, silk sheets, she ran to the bed yelling, "Oh my fucking god, I know he didn't do it…did he do it…yesssssssssssssssssssss!"

Lying on the bed was the Donna Karan, sequined, stretch jersey dress that she fell in love with last weekend. Bri could afford anything she wanted, but last month, she made a promise to herself that she would curb her spending and limit her purchases of clothing, because outside of the massive closet she had in her master suite, she had also turned two other rooms in the mansion into closets. This dress made her pussy wet but she stuck to her guns.

Rubbing her hands along the dress, she had a twinkle in her eyes as she called out for her husband. "Jasonnnnnnn. Come here baby…oh my god!"

The dress felt just as good as it looked. But the feel of arms around her waist and his tongue licking her neck as he said, "You want me baby?" Caused a small eruption between her legs.

"Umm, baby what is all of this?" Bri asked as she turned to face her very handsome husband.

Jason was decked out in his Armani best. He smelled so good she wanted to skip dinner and get right to the desert. Without answering, but with a sexy smile in his eyes, Jason placed his lips close to hers and said, "Follow me sexy."

Bri couldn't even front, this is what she loved about Jason; he knew how to make a woman feel special. She followed him into the ensuite where she could smell White Diamonds in the air. Jason winked at her, causing her to smile.

She knew Jason went out and bought the bubble bath in the scent of her favorite fragrance, thinking to herself, *This is how a man should treat his woman.*

Bri stepped into a steaming hot bubble bath just the way she liked it. Jason lit lavender-scented candles then dimmed the lights. The sexy sounds of Luther emitted through the speakers as Jason said, "Enjoy baby, I'll be back for you shortly." With that, he closed the door, leaving Bri in paradise.

Leaning back in her home away from home, Bri allowed her mind to relax. That's what happened when she was in her tub, all of her worries and fears were put to rest. The water was just the right temperature, hot enough to massage her body but not cause any real damage. The White Diamond bath salt, her absolute favorite, was increasing her pleasure. She couldn't believe Jason could still be this thoughtful; she started to feel a little guilty about how she had been feeling lately, but quickly pushed it aside. Tonight, she would enjoy her husband; she could sort her feelings out another day.

When Joe's sexy voice took over the speakers with "I Wanna Know," it added to the sensual spell Bri was under. Closing her eyes, she allowed the lyrics to enter her soul.

It's amazing how you knock me off my feet
Every time you come around me, I get weak, oh yeah
Nobody ever made me feel this way, oh
You kiss my lips and then you take my breath away
So I wanna know

After her relaxing bath, Bri got dressed in her Donna
Karan best, looked herself over in the full length mirror
and was in awe. She thought, *I mean, I know I look good,
but this dress tho; it really brings out the best in my body,
damnnnnnnnnnnn!* As she turned back and forth in the
mirror admiring herself, she silently wondered who Jason
had chosen to join them tonight; she could hear him on
the private balcony. It was always exciting when there
was a new playmate. Bri felt blessed to have a husband
that was willing to accommodate her sexual needs. Since
most men couldn't handle her lifestyle for the long run,
she felt marriage wouldn't be in the plans for her.

As she applied her makeup, she thought about all the
failed relationships with men who were down in the
beginning but eventually, jealously came in and fucked
the whole relationship up. Smacking her lips together
after applying her lipstick, she said, "But not Jason, he's
different. He enjoys the lifestyle just as much as I do.
Although I find myself getting bored with him
sometimes, nights like this make me glad I married him."

The private balcony overlooked the massive, lush green
grounds. There was a hint of red in the sky that added to
the sexy glow surrounding the illuminated candles on the
table. The table itself was beautiful, the crystal was
sparkling on the crisp, white linen, and the table was set
with rich gold china.

The theme Jason had selected was love, which shined through with the red accents on the table. As she walked out onto the balcony, Bri was in awe of the care Jason took to make this night special for her. Noticing there was only a place setting for two, she was a little confused but still amazed at the atmosphere. Jason walked up behind her smelling so good that Bri had the uncontrollable instinct to lick her lips.

Wrapping his arms around her waist, he started singing the last lines to the Usher song that was crooning though the speakers. It was the hit "My Boo," which was just how she felt, like she was being held by her boo. They rocked back and forth until the song was over. Still caught up in the bliss of it, Bri was singing, "My O, My O, My O, My O, My booooo," even after the next song started.

Jason took Bri's hand and ushered her toward her seat. Ever the gentleman, he pulled her seat out and bowed, "My lady." This made Bri grin from ear-to-ear. She really approved of his effort, but had to admit she was anxious to know what the evening entertainment would be because all of the pampering was making her pussy wet.

Dinner was more than splendid, a perfect scenario for the relaxation they both needed. Unable to curtail her excitement any longer, Bri said, "Whewww baby, I can't even begin to tell you how beautiful this was. My favorite dinner, the dress you knew I loved but was challenging myself not to buy, just the whole atmosphere you created. I absolutely love it and want you to know that."

There was a slight chill in the air but Bri was so hot it didn't even cause her to shiver. Jason smiled at his wife's compliment; it let him know that his hard work was appreciated. He hoped the remainder of the evening would go as well. He figured now was as good a time as any. He used the remote to turn the speakers down, causing Bri to give him her undivided attention.

She felt herself getting excited, but the serious expression on her husband's face was threatening to dampen her sexual mood.

"What is it Jason?" Bri asked a little lower than she would normally speak.

Clearing his throat, he kept it as real as possible. "I've had a lot on my mind for a minute." Jason exhaled as he watched Bri carefully. Licking his lips, he continued, "I'm ready for us to close the door to our open marriage."

There he had said it. He was watching closely for her reaction, but he didn't see anything. Bri was sitting there looking at him, or maybe it was through him. The entire time she was thinking, *Here we go again with this switch up shit.*

I should have known it was coming; I mean it always does. The difference now is that I fucked up and married this weak nigga. Now what the fuck do I do? Normally, I just ended the relationship and kept it pushing.

Time seemed to pass without any words being exchanged. The tension of an otherwise beautiful night got extremely uncomfortable. Jason got up from his chair and took a seat next to Bri, placing her hands in his lap.

He stared into her eyes but couldn't decipher what was on her mind. He couldn't tell if she was contemplating his statement or if she was pissed off. Just when he couldn't take it anymore, Bri removed her hands from his lap and cradled his face. Gazing deep into his eyes, she still saw remnants of the man she fell in love with. She wanted to scream at him not to change on her, but decided against it. Instead, she said, "Time for words has passed. Take me to bed and make love to me like it's the last time you'll be able to."

It wasn't the reaction Jason was looking for. Silently, he wondered if she really meant it would be the last time they made love. Shaking that thought off, he rose from his chair, pulling Bri up with him, and drew her in for a passionate kiss as he lifted her into his massive arms.

Bri wrapped her legs around his waist and deepened the kiss. Jason walked with Bri clutching his body. This was what he wanted, just him and his woman with no one else interfering. He would let the thought of a closed marriage policy marinate with Bri while he served her up a big dick with a side of tongue action that would help put things in perspective for her. Nevertheless, he had already made up his mind and that was the end of it.

Slamming the binoculars down, it was evident that watching was causing ill feelings. It was hard to witness the love Jason and Bri shared over dinner. A beautiful setting and sexy music along with plenty of laughter was simply too much. Camped out in a utility truck with sweat pouring down a face that was full of disappointment was a person who was livid. It was painfully clear that sending the texts and emails had not dulled the passion between Jason and Bri.

Staring in the rearview mirror, the reflection that was returned was one of compulsive preoccupation. Now it was time to take this obsession to the next level. Cranking the truck up, tires screeched while exiting the wealthy neighborhood. It was time to throw a monkey wrench in all of this happiness.

Marta

Two days later, there was something in the air that Marta couldn't quite put her finger on. Bri was late for work which never happens. That in itself let Marta know something was off. Sipping her water, she tried to concentrate on the proposal she was preparing for Beauty Mark, Inc. During her last meeting with Bri, she was filled in on Duke's offer. Marta had to admit, she was impressed. Scrunching up her face, she could truly say she didn't like Duke. Her feelings weren't based on anything he'd done to her personally. Actually, they were based on the fact that Bri was interested in him. Despite that, the pitch that Duke made to Glamour Girls was financially sound; therefore, Marta couldn't ignore how good it was for business. Standing up suddenly, she came from around her desk and paced the room back and forth. The plush carpet yielded the sudden activity with ease. Marta displayed a devilish grin on her face as she thought aloud, "I might just have a way to kill two birds with one stone. I can have Bri to myself and get rid of Duke and Jason."

Hastily returning to her desk, she tapped a couple of keys on her laptop then withheld a huge grin while singing, "Play that funky music white girl. Play that funky music white." This was always her theme song when she was about to put in some work.

Say What Bitch!

It was already noon and Bri wasn't in the office yet. Charmaine was on *Face book* reading Jason's post updates. She traced his face on a picture he put up yesterday of him in a grey, Brooks Brothers suit. The sexy smile that looked back at her appeared to be just for her; at least that's how she saw it. Charmaine was tired of waiting for him to come to her, so she decided it was time to go to him. She had it all planned out, but couldn't put it into play until Bri came to work. Checking her watch, it was now almost one; shaking her head, she said, "Something must be wrong because Bri is a stickler about being on time; she better not be fucking my man I know that." Charmaine or Charm buggy as her *Face book* name read got loss in her own thoughts as she clicked on Jason's pictures. The buzzing of her office phone put a halt to her fantasy world. She was pissed about being disturbed while spending time with her boo. Picking up the phone, her tone reflected her frustration as she screamed, "What!"

Bri pulled the phone away from her ear and stared at it for a quick second. She was sure she didn't hear her assistant just yell into the damn phone.

Bri shook her head as she thought; *This chick has no clue that I'm not the one to be fucked with today. Her ass can be gone.* Putting the phone back to her ear and taking a breath, she said as professionally as possible, "Whatever has got your thong in a twist, you better get it outcha ass. Now bring the signature report to my office and leave your attitude in yours!" Shaking her head, Bri slammed the phone down then walked over to her floor-length window.

Looking out, she smiled inside; Glamour Girls was located in one of the largest buildings in Downtown Norfolk. It wasn't the New York or California scene, but Glamour Girls put Norfolk on the cosmetic map. While gazing out into the pretty blue ski, she let her anger over Charmaine's foolishness subside as she remembered her early morning meeting.

With the proposed merger between Beauty Mark, Inc. and Glamour Girls, Inc, Bri was planning to move from being the largest makeup distributor of African American beauty products in the United States to the largest distributor of beauty products period.

She had a meeting at the Oceanfront Hilton first thing this morning to hammer out the particulars. She walked into the meeting feeling and looking like a million bucks.

The burnt orange pencil skirt hugged her hips just right. She wore a wrapped, silk, crisp, white blouse that made the outfit look professional with a hint of sexy. What took her breath away were the ghost white, Señora T-Strap Open Toe Christian Louboutins. If you were a shoe whore like Bri, you couldn't help but strut in them.

She had Marta running the numbers on the deal with BM; she also scheduled Marta to meet with Lance, the financial assistant at BM. It was Bri's intention to get a little more information up close and personal to gauge the atmosphere of the proposal, or at least that's what she told herself. Sitting across from Duke in a room full of families enjoying their morning meal just felt right. In Bri's mind, this man was fine as hell and wore confidence like a second skin.

With the curve ball Jason had just put on the table, Bri was thinking about adding a little more flexibility into her life, thinking to herself,

Don't get me wrong, I love my husband, but if he thinks only having sex with him is going to be enough to keep the fire burning in our marriage, he has missed his guess. I told his ass that before we got married and I meant what the hell I said.

More determined than ever to make her own indecent proposal, Bri smiled as she turned her undivided attention toward the sexiness before her.

Marta's voice coming across her private intercom disrupted her hypnotic state before she could get to the good part. An instant frown was quickly replaced as she turned from the window to tend to business. Marta asked Bri to come to the main conference room; her voice sounded funny again. Prepared to put out whatever fire that might have been brewing, Bri got up from her desk, thinking to herself, *Marta better get onboard with this game plan or she's going to be left in the dust.*

Dis Bitch

Charmaine entered Bri's office, attempting to hide her attitude, carrying the report that her highness demanded. Glancing around, she was instantly pissed off. Despite all the hoopla, Bri wasn't even in her office. "It's just like her to make demands then dip," she said as she started walking toward the desk to leave the report. Charmaine hated how plush Bri's office was. Looking around, she noted that the furniture was the best in quality. There was a spacious u-shaped executive marble desk, two leather sofas, and a seating area for eight. Moving around the desk, Charmaine's eyes were drawn to the massive windows because the views from Bri's office were breathtaking. To the left, there was an opening to a 1,000 square foot furnished patio. Staring at the patio while shaking her head, Charmaine remembered the photo shoot that was held on that very patio last year to highlight Glamour Girls' products, not to mention the many cocktail parties that Bri hosted for new clients.

Luther's version of, "If This World Were Mine," began to play loudly on Bri's phone as her ringtone, just as Charmaine placed the report on her desk.

Charmaine couldn't believe Bri had left her phone, because she always had it glued to her ear. Glancing toward the door to ensure no one was coming, Charmaine picked up the phone and immediately smiled as she saw Jason, the object of her passion, in nothing but his boxer briefs flash across the screen. The picture was absolute perfection in Charmaine's mind. Just as quickly as the good feeling washed over her, the smile turned into a frown as she focused on the name listed under her man's picture was *hubby*.

"I can't believe dis bitch still claiming my man; I don't care if she is married to him, he belongs to me; but she'll see, real soon." Charmaine spit the words out with venom as she tossed the phone back on the desk then searched through the drawers. Before exiting the room, she embraced the attitude she had previously tried to disguise.

Drama's Breeze

Now that he was back in his office, Duke felt like he could let out the breath he had been holding in for what seemed like forever. That's how being with Bri made him feel, like he was the most important man in the world. He was mad at himself because he tried over the years to avoid her for this very reason; she was irresistible. To some degree, Duke was ashamed of himself. Bri was testing his moral values and he didn't know how to stop her. The fact that she was another man's wife was hard for Duke to dismiss. He had met Jason several times when he was working on commercials for BM. Before it was public knowledge that Jason and Bri were an item, Duke was really considering making his move. He only fell back because Jason was a straight shooter and appeared to be an all-around good guy. Two years later, he didn't know what to feel. The more he saw Bri, the more he contemplated changing some of his personal practices. Watching her walk toward him in the fitted, orange skirt made his body betray him. All he wanted to do was book a room and make sweet love to her all day.

It was Duke's suggestion that they meet for breakfast. He wanted Bri out of her natural habitat of computers, phones, and employees. The main goal of the meeting was to work out the particulars of the merger. New York Fashion Week was approaching soon which made a smooth merger transition even more important. Over breakfast, they discussed exactly what a BM and Glamour Girls company would look like as well as what new cosmetic products BM could bring to the table to add to the Glamour Girls line.

BM would focus on mainstream beauty products and Glamour Girls would continue to kill the black beauty market. They kicked around a new company name Glamour Beauty Girls, Inc. Bri was warming up to the name. Duke expressed the main benefit of the merger was so the new company could secure all the endorsements and distribution during the fashion season.

Over the last three years, Glamour Girls had the cosmetic distribution endorsement for the entire New York Fashion Week season. Fashion week was held in February and September of each year.

There were a multitude of fashion productions around town during that time, including Mercedes-Benz Fashion Week and MADE Fashion Week. Bri had the lockdown on all the cosmetics used at those large venues in addition to all of the independent fashion productions around town. Now it was time to go after a new fashion season. Merging with BM would open up the door to the other three large fashion weeks around the world. Together, they were known as "The Big Four," and Bri was making small waves at attempting to secure the market. BM had a larger following overseas, which would give them a better shot at Fashion Week for Paris, London, and Milan. The merger would make GBG the largest cosmetic house in the world.

As he punched numbers on his keyboard, Duke frowned. He knew his mother wouldn't be happy about the merger. Her preference was Beauty Mark go to war with Glamour Girls to regain their footing in the black beauty market. Duke was more forward thinking; company growth and longevity was his main course of business.

He wasn't prepared to succumb to the old way of doing business. Instead, he decided to be innovative. This merger would launch Beauty Mark into a new stratosphere.

His phone buzzed then his personal assistant, Jon Jon's voice came through the speaker sounding a little funny. "Duke, there's a Startisha Duke here to see you."

Duke just stared at the speaker; he knew who Startisha was. Over the years, he had tried very hard to push her out of his mind. Acknowledging her existence made his father's betrayal real, which made his blood boil beyond healthy levels. He saw her whenever he opened a non-descript fashion magazine to do some much needed reading. Duke had to stay up-to-date with what was new in fashion. Even though she had the looks of a prized runway model, the big dogs wouldn't touch her. Duke rubbed his temples to ward off the headache that he felt creeping up as his mind wandered back to the first and last time he had seen Startisha Duke.

It was a beautiful and sad day all wrapped into one. Yes, today was the day Poppa Duke was to be buried. Nevertheless, the Duke Family refused to permit anyone to be somber on this day; it wasn't what his father wanted. Duke knew his pops wanted good music to be played and to have his devoted and loving family surrounding him. Although his death was sudden, he talked to his only son about what he wanted when his time came. He wrote out specific instructions and planned out every step, well almost. Poppa Duke was sixty-five years young, but smoking and drinking over the years destroyed his body internally.

However, his brilliant mind functioned until the end. Duke was thirty-five and already groomed to take over much of the family business. Hence, Poppa Duke made sure he knew what to do in case of an emergency.

The family was ushered through the vestibule of Mount Carmel Baptist Church. This was the family's church; the head pastor was Damion Duke, his uncle. The church was packed with friends, family, industry people, and even enemies of Poppa Duke. As Duke assisted his elderly mother to her seat, he nodded his head to people he recognized. He saw his cousin Lance and London, twins who were as close to him as siblings.

He noticed how sad London looked, so he gave her a heartfelt smile to cheer her up. That's how Duke was; he always wanted his family to be happy.

The organist started playing and everyone took their seat. Uncle Duke was standing at the podium looking out at his loving family. Duke looked deeply into his eyes and gave him a strong head nod. Duke knew his uncle was expecting him to step into his father's shoes in business and as head of the household. Silently, Duke was assuring him he would do his best. Sister Odessa started singing "Amazing Grace," Mahalia Jackson's version. She knew this to be Poppa Duke's favorite hymn. Oftentimes, Poppa Duke spoke of what he called the "Negro Spiritual," and how the song expressed the joy felt as a result of being delivered from slavery or misery. He had her sing the song often; today would be no different.

The Home going was beautiful. People made awesome tributes to his father, many of which touched his heart. Apparently, one more person wanted to make a tribute; she was approaching the podium slowly, but definitely with a purpose. From what Duke could see, she appeared to be young, maybe 13 or so.

He looked at his mother, who was wiping her eyes with a handkerchief; she didn't even notice the girl. Duke could tell she was beautiful, but he couldn't place her.

When she made it to the mic, she looked out at the crowd and was noticeably crying. Her voice contradicted her somber appearance. She sounded self-assured as she spoke into the mic. "First, giving honor to God, who is the head of my life, Pastor Duke, and fellow saints. The passing of Poppa Duke is a very sad day for all of us."

Duke sat up a little straighter in his pew as the girl spoke. Although she looked very young, she sounded extremely mature. He wanted to know which parishioner's child this was as she continued with tears running down her cheeks. "My name is Startisha..." After taking a short pause, she continued, "Startisha Duke. I'm the youngest child of Poppa Duke." Startisha stared directly in her brother's face as she spoke.

A collective gasp could be heard throughout the church. Duke looked deeply into the girl's eyes as she said the words. In them, he saw truth.

Momma Duke jumped up from her pew quicker than her sixty-three years should allow and screamed, "Liar...you filthy black Liar!"

The church was in an uproar after Momma Duke's statement. A beautiful black woman, regal in appearance jumped up from her pew and ran to Startisha, who fell in her arms, sobbing uncontrollably. People were yelling and pointing toward Momma Duke. Uncle Duke could be heard on the microphone trying to calm everyone down. Grabbing his mother by the hand, Duke ushered her into the back of the church where his uncle's office was located. He couldn't believe his mother had made an outburst like that. Never once had he heard her talk about black or white and it disturbed him. He sat his mother down on the cream, leather couch as gently as he could. She was babbling about telling the truth and love, most of which Duke couldn't make out.

"Momma rest back here and let me help Uncle Duke clear the church out. I'll get to the bottom of this." He rubbed her cheek, wiping away the tears that continued to flow as she babbled. Duke wasn't even sure if she heard him, but since she was safe, he left her sitting on the couch and went back into the sanctuary.

Uncle Duke did a good job of clearing most of the people out, but the nosey ones were still sticking around.

Approaching his uncle and a couple of his cousins who were scheduled to be pallbearers, Duke stated, "I want to bury my father with as much of his dignity intact as I can. So let's proceed to the burial site and put him to rest. There's nothing more we can do about what happened here today, but my father deserves respect."

No one was in disagreement with Duke; they all had nothing but the utmost respect for him. Uncle Duke wanted his brother laid to rest. They would deal with the indiscretion later. Peering around the church until he spotted his cousin London, Duke motioned for her to come over. She approached him with tears still in her eyes and her arms outstretched. She was the epitome of a beautiful woman; he knew Uncle Duke was proud of her. London was a Harvard trained corporate lawyer, single, with no kids. "Duke, I am so sorry it turned out like this. Poppa Duke doesn't deserve this no matter what he had going on in his personal life." London hugged her big cousin tightly.

Smiling, Duke inhaled his cousin's cologne, something that felt normal because she always smelled good. Since he didn't know what he was about to endure, right now, he needed normal.

"Thank you cuzzo; I know I can always count on you and Lance. We're about to go bury my daddy. I need you to go to the back, get momma, and make sure she makes it to the gravesite. She's not doing too well, so be prepared." Before he turned and started giving instructions to the rest of his family, Duke smiled and gave his little cousin a quick peck on the cheek. He was determined to lay his father in his grave with as much dignity as possible.

The sun was beating down on the gravesite like it was angry. Duke was surprised to see so many people. He couldn't be sure if they were there to see his father laid to rest or if they were hoping for more theatrics.

Either way, Duke was determined that things would go smoothly. Checking his watch as he looked across the grassy null for his mother, she still wasn't there.

After twenty minutes and no answer from either her nor London's phone, Duke couldn't ask people to continue to stand out in the treacherous heat, so he reluctantly gave the go ahead for his Uncle to begin the internment.

The family decided to cancel the traditional dinner that followed most burials. All Duke wanted to do was locate his mother; he knew she was upset.

For that reason, he was worried about her. He saw Lance moving hurriedly in his direction, which was an immediate cause for concern. Lance was similar to London in ambition, but was easygoing and extremely laid-back. He didn't get worked up over much, so if he was fast-walking toward Duke, he knew something was up. Before Lance could even catch his breath, Duke was already asking him what was up. "Lance, tell me something good man." Duke had an uneasy expression on his face as he awaited the answer.

Lance was still holding his cell phone gripped tightly in his hands as he attempted to catch his breath. "London called me; she's at King's Daughters hospital with Momma Duke." He had a look of sorrow on his face; there was something he wasn't saying.

Duke didn't have time to get answers. He had just lost his father and now his mother was in the hospital. He took off running across the grass with Lance and Uncle Duke close on his heels.

*Before they could catch up, he had hoped in the
limousine and peeled away from the gravesite. The limo
driver could be seen running behind the limo in the
rearview mirror. Duke didn't give a fuck about that; he
was worried about losing his mother too. His heart was
beating so fast, it felt as though it would burst. His entire
existence was intertwined with his parents and their
legacy. To ask him, an only child, to endure another
dramatic loss was too much for him to comprehend. He
was speeding as he turned into the circular driveway of
the emergency room. There was a loud thump near the
rear of the limo; he was certain he had run over
something or someone. Duke barely put the limo in park
before he jumped out and sprinted through the hospital
door.*

*London spotted him coming through the door, looking
scared and confused. Quickly, she jumped up and ran in
his direction.*

*"Duke! Duke, I'm over here!" That's all she could get
out before he ran over and swept her up in his strong
arms.*

*Duke's nerves were on edge; he needed to gain control,
so he released his cousin and got himself together. "How
is momma?" He inquired in a voice that belied how
frightened he was.*

*London let the tears flow freely as she said, "The doctors
haven't told me anything yet. But when I went to my
dad's office to get her, she was lying on the floor
shaking. I called an ambulance then I tried to reach you
but my calls went unanswered."*

Taking in everything his cousin said, Duke turned to go to the nurses' station when he saw a doctor walking toward him. So he stopped in his tracks. "Doctor, can you give me some information on Madeline Duke?" Duke stood in the doctor's path as he attempted to pass him.

The doctor looked the man over then gazed around the room as if he was looking for someone in particular before he said in a condescending voice,

"I'm looking for Mrs. Duke's family. Excuse me sir." He attempted to move around Duke.

Realizing what he was dealing with, Duke got agitated but tried to keep himself calm. "I am Hudson Duke. Mrs. Duke is my mother. Is that family enough for you?" Duke watched as the color drained from the doctor's face.

The doctor whose name tag read, Dr. Blizzard quickly tried to recover from his prejudice actions.

"I'm so sorry Mr. Duke; I just wanted to make sure I was disseminating information to the entire family. Mrs. Duke has suffered a major stroke with acute neurological symptoms."

Before he could continue, Duke stopped him to ensure he understood exactly what he was saying. He wasn't going to allow Dr. Blizzard to speed through his explanation. "Ok doctor, so she's had a stroke, but is she conscious and is she going to be fine?" Duke asked the questions unsure if he was ready for the answers.

Dr. Blizzard could see the hurt and concern in the young man's face. He felt kind of bad about letting his prejudice shine through in such a delicate situation. He tried to soften his face and his tone of voice.

"I'm sorry for what you're going through Mr. Duke. And to answer your question, yes, your mother is conscious; she has numbness on her right side and stiffness in her neck. You can see her, but be prepared because her speech is very slurred and she may sleep in the middle of your visit. She's in room D5." With that, the doctor pointed in the direction of the room then excused himself, scurrying away hastily in the opposite direction.

Standing over his mother, watching her chest go up and down as she slept, Duke said a silent prayer that she was still among the living. As if burying her husband, her partner of 36 years wasn't taxing enough, she was also faced with the possibility that her husband was living a double life. Duke was sure that a mixture of those events was the reason his mother was lying in a hospital room with her face looking slightly contorted. Rubbing her sterling silver hair away from her face, Duke whispered to his mother,

"Hey sweet lady, you don't have my permission to leave me. I couldn't make it here without you. Rest today, but tomorrow I want you back home nagging me to death." Duke kissed his mother's cheek then turned to leave the room. When he made it back to the waiting room, he stopped dead in his tracks.

There London was, arguing with the regal looking black lady from the funeral. And standing alone was the pretty little lady that called herself Startisha Duke.

Jon Jon screaming through the speaker jarred Duke from his daydream. Jon Jon was a little on the flamboyant side, but he was an excellent personal assistant. After Momma Duke got sick, Duke really needed someone reliable, consistent, and knowledgeable.

Jon Jon was a lowly clerk in the distribution office, but one day, he was sitting outside of Duke's door dressed to the nines with his resume in hand. Duke liked his spunk, but advised him to turn the volume down a notch and they would do a trial run. That was five years ago and one of the smartest decisions Duke had ever made since he took over the day-to-day operations.

"Duke, are you ok? Don't make me come in there because you know I will." Jon Jon had to laugh at himself because he knew Duke was gonna go off on him.

Duke could only shake his head at the speaker.

He knew he'd better answer because Jon Jon would indeed barge into his office to make sure things were ok. For some reason, he fancied himself to be Duke's protector.

At first, Duke was put off by the special attention. He even addressed it once but Jon Jon put Duke right in his place when he said, *Duke, I am gay not desperate. You are no more my type than a man in the moon. But what you are to me is family.* Duke chuckled to himself as he remembered that.

"Jon Jon, I'm here so hold your horses and send the young lady in." Duke responded through the speaker as he prepared himself to deal with the inevitable.

Devil On Your Shoulder
Lost in thought, Jason was sitting in his office with a view of the Chesapeake Bay. It was strange how the icy blue water had a way of organizing one's thoughts. It had only been a couple of days since he gave Bri the ultimatum, but you would think they had never had the conversation. Bri had been avoiding any contact with him, staying at the office late, using the excuse that she was preparing for the meeting with the New York Fashion Board. Jason had been with Bri long enough to know there was a lot of work that went into the preparation, but it never stopped her from being an attentive wife. Jason recognized that she was avoiding him; he had already tried to call her three times today and left a message but had gotten no reply. Despite how much he didn't want to admit it, he was hurt. Jason shook his head as he sat in a trance. At this point, there was no denying that he wasn't sure where his marriage stood. The new message notification sounded on his cell phone. Jason turned his attention from the solitude of the water to click the new message. He was silently hoping Bri wanted to meet at home for an afternoon snack.

Unfortunately, sex with his wife was one of the casualties as a result of his ultimatum.

Problems at home? Time to let that bitch go and let me takeover.

Jason threw his iPhone across the room before he thought about it. He was so sick of this bitch playing on his phone. Despite what was going on with him and his wife, he would not replace her for some random bitch.

63

Jason placed his head in his hands, trying to figure out how a happy home had come to this. The other question he needed to figure out was who this person was and how they knew what he was going through in his home. Jason decided the best way to catch a bitch was to play pussy. He jumped up from his chair to retrieve his iPhone, silently thanking God that he didn't shatter it. Retrieving the message, he re-read it twice as he thought about how he wanted to proceed. A sly grin spread across his face as he decided on a course of action. *It would be good to have someone to talk to who has my best interest in mind. I don't know how to feel right now, can we meet?*

Jason almost burst out laughing when he hit the send button. He felt happy, like he was accomplishing something. It had been a couple of days since he felt this useful. Yes, there were problems in his marriage, but he felt like all marriages hit rough patches. What Jason didn't agree with was someone trying to infiltrate his marriage. He would deal with this problem then he would re-address the issues in his home. At the end of the day, he just wanted his woman back. The notification chime went off and Jason quickly clicked on the new message. *Bout time you see things my way. Yes let's meet.*

The arrogance of the chick behind the text was not lost on Jason as he thought to himself, *This bitch really thinks someone wants her stalkish ass. What she don't know is I'm gonna put my foot in her ass for fucking with my family.* Jason's mind was ticking as he typed in his reply. *Name the place and the time and I will definitely be there.*

For a minute, he felt a little guilty. Even though he didn't have any malicious intent, he was still going to meet a woman he knew had a crush on him. If Bri found out, she might think he was trying to fuck the chick.

Subconsciously, he began to get angry with himself for giving a fuck about how Bri was feeling. She was avoiding him–not talking to him, not fucking him. Shit, she had basically abandoned him. The side of him that used to not give a fuck about a bitch's feelings was telling him to get some pussy. Jason was feeling a little dizzy. He felt like he could honestly feel a little devil dressed in red on one shoulder and a little, white angel on the other. The question was which one he would listen to.

Reach For The Stars

Bri couldn't contain her excitement about the upcoming fashion season. Normally, she was reserved, but the possibility of Glamour Girls being the preferred cosmetics company for the entire fashion season was something to rave about. This move would catapult her vision for her company into a new stratosphere. She had to prepare to present Glamour Girls' cosmetic catalog to the fashion week board in NYC. Bri reasoned with herself that this merger would add nicely to the overall catalog. The expertise of Beauty Mark in the mainstream cosmetic market, coupled with Glamour Girls' choke hold on the African American beauty market was nothing short of brilliant. These were the thoughts on her mind as she sat across the conference room table from her partner in crime. Marta didn't have an outward appearance of being excited; she actually looked preoccupied. "Marta, what's so important that you dragged me down here in a rush?" Bri asked in a chipper voice.

Looking up from the mountain of papers that she had on the table, Marta gave Bri a sly look. She wanted to talk some sense into Bri. She wanted Glamour Girls to stay independent.

She didn't want Bri working closely with Hudson Duke. Marta was aware that her issues weren't based on anything real; she was simply jealous. Shuffling the papers around on the table, she finally spoke. "I think the merger is a bad idea and will hurt the company's bottom line." Marta looked into Bri's eyes, hoping to gauge how she was taking the information. Usually, it was difficult to read Bri, but today she was an open book.

It was apparent that she was gung ho about the merger and unhappy about Marta's resistance. Marta didn't care; she just wanted Duke out of the picture and for Bri to finally see her as a viable sex partner.

Silence lingered in the atmosphere of the conference room. Bri was watching Marta put her selfishness before the prosperity and growth of HER business. Marta had been there from the conception. However, she was not the owner of the company.

Her contribution to the company could not be denied, but at the end of the day, she was hired help.

Bri kept her personal as well as professional life very separate for this exact reason. Marta was allowing her personal feelings for Bri to cloud her professional judgment. Bri could see it in her eyes and her sentiments.

She had been planning to address it, but with everything going on, it slipped her mind. The time to air the shit out was right now. Raising her hands and slamming them on the table, Bri got Marta's undivided attention.

"Marta, for months, you have been walking around here like a lovesick puppy and it stops now!" The force in Bri's delivery could not be overlooked. "You are very important to me. I think of you like a sister I never had. But that's as far as it goes or will ever go. I'm not even gonna say I'm flattered because I'm not. What I want is you to do the job I pay you for and leave the rest of that bullshit at home. Can you do that?" Bri had her fingertips spread on the table as she emphasized each of her points.

Marta's cheeks were bright red. She never expected Bri to go off on her, now she was really in her feelings and doing a poor job at hiding it. Marta felt like she was a crucial part of this company and was irreplaceable, even if she wasn't a CEO. She had been there from day one when there was nothing but a dream and ambition. Right now, her head was hurting and her heart was pounding in her chest as her mind raced with thoughts of, *This is one selfish bitch! I AM THIS COMPANY!*

Grabbing the glass of water that was in front of her, her trembling hands were hard to miss. Nonetheless, she made sure to drink some of the water to calm herself down before she spoke. The coolness of the water had the intended effect as she placed the glass back on the table and took a deep breath. "Bri, I don't know what to say." She was shaking her head and holding back tears that she didn't want to fall as she continued. "I have never done anything to damage the company and my feelings for you have never come before business. The fact that you're going off on me proves my point that this deal is not good for business."

By holding up her hand for her to stop, Bri interrupted her before she could continue. There was no way that Bri planned to sit through the bullshit, there was way too much work to be done. She was patting her suit jacket for her phone, not sure what she did with it. Then she started gathering the papers regarding the deal and got up from the table. She looked at Marta with an expression that was a cross between disappointment and amusement as she said, "By the end of the day, I want to know your game plan for following through with the meeting with Lance Duke.

If you can't do it, then I expect your resignation on my desk by 5 p.m. Capiche?" With that, she turned to leave the conference room. She didn't feel bad about how she dealt with Marta, because business was no place for her petty infatuations. Bri felt she had to nip that shit in the bud before it got out of hand. On her way, she let the door slam, leaving Marta sitting at the table with a stupid expression on her face.

Making it back to her office, Bri was in a funky mood. She just didn't have room in her life for anymore foolishness.

Things in her personal life were getting out-of-hand; she felt as though her normal balance was off. Avoiding her husband could only go on for so long, she was going to have to face him and make some decisions. Walking over to her desk, Bri could see that Charmaine had left the reports that she needed. She made a mental note to peek in on her and see what was going on with her. It wasn't like Charmaine to act funky. For that reason, Bri wanted to make sure to address it rather than let it fester as she thought to herself, *I already got one employee acting a damn fool. I'll fuck around and clean house in this bitch.* Placing the report back on her desk, Bri noticed her phone sitting next to her computer.

She quickly grabbed it to see if she had any missed calls from Duke. Realizing she was hoping to hear from Duke and not Jason, she shook her head and had to chuckle to herself. There were three missed calls and one voicemail logged on her screen, but neither of them were from Duke. In fact, all three were from Jason.

Sighing heavily, Bri sat in her comfortable chair and dialed her voicemail to retrieve her messages.

Baby, we need to talk. Avoiding the issue is only complicating it. I need you, but I'm not gonna beg you. So I'ma leave the ball in your court. Take this with you while you're thinking, I genuinely love you and that's not easy to find.

The call ended, leaving Bri sitting in her plush office with tears in her eyes. It wasn't that she didn't love Jason because she did. Most women wouldn't even understand her feelings when it came to men, but it was truly ingrained deep in her psyche. Through her tears, Bri thought about growing up in a household that made her question her womanhood and sexuality.

When Briann was fifteen, her childhood innocence was interrupted by tragedy. Before that, her life was not the storybook tale that most people thought. As an only child, she always felt she was a disappointment to her father. He often said to her that he wished she had been a boy. He never spent any time with her like other fathers did with their children. Briann didn't know what to do with the sadness she felt inside, so she escaped into the fairytale world of reading.

Even though her mother encouraged her hobby, she did nothing to change the circumstances. In reality, there wasn't anything she could do. She suffered just as much verbal and emotional abuse as Briann did. Briann often heard her mother crying in the middle of the night. There were many arguments that she overheard when everyone thought she was asleep.

From those arguments, Briann learned that her father was unapologetically unfaithful. He blamed her mother for his failures. She even heard her father call his mother bitches and hoes. On these nights, she found herself wishing he was dead. The worst thing about all of it was watching her mother continually try to please her father. The more she tried, the more blatant his abuse became. Although it was never physical, it might as well have been because her mother's appearance began to resemble a woman who had been beaten down.

Outwardly, she looked ragged and her self-esteem was completely demolished. Caring for Briann was probably the only thing keeping her sane, but after a while that wasn't enough.

The day her life changed forever started just like any other. She woke up, got dressed for school, and ate her breakfast. The house was quiet, but it usually was early in the morning. Most nights, her mother stayed up until the wee hours crying while her father was out in the streets. By the time the alarm went off at 6 a.m., her mother was finally asleep but her father hadn't made it home from his night in the streets. Briann made it a habit of getting herself off to school in the right frame of mind. On this day, she was feeling hopeful; she felt things were going to change for the better. Having received her report card from school that showed a vast improvement in her grades. Therefore, after school, she ran home to show her mother what she'd accomplished. She was feeling really good.

When she entered her home, she knew something was wrong. Everything looked exactly like it did when she left that morning. That was strange, usually when she got home, her mother was cooking dinner and cleaning the house. This was their special time before her father got home and ruined everything.

Moving slowly down the hallway, Briann smelled a strange odor. The closer she got to her mother's bedroom, the stronger the odor became. She called out for her mother, scared to open the door when she didn't get an answer. Conversely, she was afraid not to. Deep inside, Briann knew this was not going to end well. She tried to trick herself into thinking if she turned around and walked back out the house, she could possibly change what her heart was telling her was about to happen. But at fifteen, she was far from a child; she understood life and unfortunately, death.

Pushing the door open, she entered the room and immediately covered her mouth. The pungent odor was almost overwhelming. The tears were already traveling down her face before her brain and heart began to communicate. Briann didn't have to be an adult to know that her mother was dead. She ran over to the bed yelling her mother's name. Her mother looked like she was sleeping, but the paleness of her skin made the tragedy a reality.

It was hard for Briann to catch her breath through her sobbing and the heaving of her chest. She sank to the floor, trying to come to grips with the fact that the one person who loved her was gone. While on the floor, she noticed a prescription pill bottle.

Picking it up, she wiped away the tears and read the name. It was her mother's prescription for Prozac; the bottle was empty and Briann didn't know what to do next. She realized she needed to call someone, but she didn't want to talk to her dad. Standing quickly, she began to look all around the room for the cordless phone. Her vision was blurry which added to her frantic movements. Normally, her mother kept the phone on the dresser. When Briann reached for the phone, she used her blouse to wipe her face, and that's when she saw her name in large print. There was a notepad sitting right next to the phone, so she reached for that instead. It was a letter from her mother.

I'm tired baby. My mind, my body, my heart, my soul is tired. I know you're sad but don't be, it's my time. Don't be mad at your father, he really is a good man deep down inside.

I know that he loves me and you too. I want you to take good care of him. You are so much stronger than I am, and I know you will be a wonderful wife and mother one day. Please remember that. I love you. Mom

Briann read the letter over and over again. No matter how many times she read it, she couldn't understand why her mother would take her own life. Picking up the phone, she dialed 911 and reported her version of what she found when the operator answered. "911, what's your emergency?" Through tears and sobs, Briann relayed to the operator that she came home and found her mother dead in her sleep.

Thinking about that time in her life only made her tears fall harder. She recalled taking the pill bottle and letter and hiding them in her backpack. She didn't want anyone to know that her mother cared so little about her that she killed herself. When her father found out her mother was dead, he quickly told Briann she would have to start earning her keep around the house. He went on and on about how he was going to cash out on the insurance policy.

She cracked a smile when she thought about how upset he was when he discovered he wasn't the beneficiary on any of her policies. Her mother's death was ruled natural, primarily because Briann removed the evidence. For that reason, she was set to inherit three hundred thousand dollars on her twenty-first birthday. Pissed, her father sent her to live with her mother's sister. He said he wasn't raising no more bitches.

Briann never knew why her father hated her so much, but she promised herself she would never give herself to one man so he could manipulate and use her the way her father did her mother. She promised herself she would possess her own mind, body, and soul. Thus, Briann focused on her future and built a wall around her heart. To date, no man has yet to climb all the way over that wall.

Startisha

The penthouse suite of the Beauty Mark office didn't look like she thought it would. She was expecting elegance and opulence, what she got instead was a regular business office with nice décor–not the extravagance she felt went hand-in-hand with the Duke name. Her father had spent thirty years making sure that the Duke name rang bells in the cosmetic world. Relaxing on the empress white, leather sofa, Startisha's mind was spinning rapidly.

Startisha Jauwel Duke was stunning in her black and white stretch knit Roberto Cavalli dress. She added a sharp A-line blazer to give her outfit a more business appropriate feel. At eighteen, she was making a living as a fresh face in editorial modeling; she wanted her face to appear on the cover of Vogue, Elle, Glamour, and Cosmo. She had dreams of putting designers on the map by wearing what the magazines pegged as the next trend in fashion. Although she was doing okay, editorial work wasn't paying as well as high fashion modeling. Startisha believed she was destined to be a runway model.

The problem was instead of helping her, the Duke name was hurting her. Most magazines wouldn't hire her because they didn't want to be on her big brother's shit list. Startisha believed with a name like Duke the world owed her.

Shifting her weight on the softest couch she had ever sat on, Startisha was feeling slightly uncomfortable. She was here to visit her older brother; however, she wasn't looking to receive a warm reception. The last time she saw her brother was at the reading of their father's will.

Even though she was only thirteen, she detected that her very presence caused turmoil.

Startisha thought losing her father was one of the most difficult things a thirteen year old girl could ever experience. Possibly causing his mean wife to have a stroke made her feel bad as well. Today was the reading of Poppa Duke's will, so Startisha was preparing, once again, to face her other family. Her mother, Glenda, didn't want her to go. She was very protective of her daughter. However, Startisha was headstrong like her father. She felt it was time that she stopped being hidden like she was a mistake. She wanted the Dukes to know who she was, because she sure knew who they were.

Sitting in the large conference room in a downtown law firm, Startisha stared at various people in the room. She recognized her big brother, Hudson, and her Uncle, Duke. She also recognized her uncle's kids, Lance and London. The side door opened and the men at the table jumped up from their seats. Startisha turned to see a pleasantly dressed woman pushing Momma Duke in a wheelchair. Startisha must have jumped slightly because her mother held her hand soothingly and she began to calm down. The further into the room the wheelchair was pushed, the worst Startisha began to feel internally.

A man that she realized was an attorney tapped a small microphone that was built into the conference table and spoke. "Now that everyone is here, let me introduce myself. I am Jeremey Anderson, Harry Duke's personal as well as estate attorney.

He has left me a number of instructions when it comes to his personal estate, one of which is that you all gather here today to listen to a letter he prepared prior to the reading of the will."

Attorney Anderson removed sheets of typed paper from his folder then began to read aloud.

Everyone in the room was staring at each other as the attorney spoke. There was a confused expression on every face in the room.

"If you're all assembled in one place that means I'm dead. Wow, I guess I knew it had to happen at some point! I want to thank each of you for being a wonderful part of my life. Upon my death, certain truths will be revealed that may cast a shadow in your hearts about how you felt about me and the life I lived. By now, I'm sure you've all met Startisha and Glenda. I know this because Startisha is too headstrong to stay away from her Poppa's funeral. Hudson, she's a lot like you in that way."

Startisha could feel every eye on her, but the only individual she was concerned with was her big brother. Making eye contact with him, she gave him a small smile, which he didn't return. Uncertain of how to feel about it, she turned her attention back to the lawyer.

"I know I have hurt my lovely wife but it was never my intent. By happenstance, I was a man in love with two women. Glenda has been a part of my life since I was a little boy and Madeline is well aware of who she is.

77

What Madeline didn't know was I never stopped loving Glenda, nor did she know we were raising a beautiful little girl together."

Once again, Startisha felt like every eye in the room was on her. Her mother was squeezing her hand firmly. It was apparent that she was feeling uncomfortable as well. Startisha squeezed her hand back. She was going to be strong for her mother, like she always was. Even at thirteen, she knew her mother was the weak link. Startisha was pissed that her mother let her father hide her away like she was something dirty. It didn't matter that Startisha had the best of everything, she was still a secret to the world and she hated that.

"At this point, I am unconcerned about how the world sees me, my legacy is intact. I have given everything I can to my children, Hudson and Startisha. In death, I want to give them each other. I curse anyone who denies me that in death.

Now to the reason you all are here—my estate. First, please understand that anyone who contests my will is to be immediately disqualified from inheriting anything.

My lawyer has the necessary paperwork to file and he will not hesitate to do so. I have left substantial endowments for both my wife and Glenda. This is to include stocks, bonds, and property.

Hudson, I am so very proud of the man you have grown into; you have soaked up the knowledge that your mother and I have given you. As majority owner of Beauty Mark, I will all of my company shares and resources to you. I know you will continue my legacy."

Gazing around the room, everyone appeared to be deep in thought. Startisha was happy that her father had provided for her mother in his will. Financially, she was totally dependent on him. Although she had a small insurance policy that he had given her years ago, fiscally, things were tight. When she heard her name, she returned her attention to the attorney.

"Startisha, my bundle of joy. You are a spitfire just like your Poppa. That can either do you well in life or cause you extreme harm. Hudson is going to be in need of a family attorney for our business. In order to give you a solid foundation, here is what I want for you.

I want you to enroll in law school, preferably Regent University, but a law school all the same. Upon your graduation and passing of the bar, I want you to join the legal team for Beauty Mark. Since I know you, I know your lips are turned up. But understand this, your inheritance will be withheld and collecting interest until you complete law school. Hudson will be the trustee over the account and will pay for your tuition and living expenses. I want you to be a part of this company, but I also want you to be self-sufficient and a law degree will ensure that."

Once again, everyone was staring at her. Even at her age, Startisha realized exactly what her dad had done. If she didn't go to law school, she wouldn't receive her inheritance. Although college was far off, she was certain she didn't want to be an attorney. She wanted to be a famous model. She wanted her name in lights. She wanted people to know who she was. She was a DUKE! She felt like her father was still trying to hide her away.

Pissed, she jumped up from her chair and ran out of the conference room. Her mother ran behind her.

The man behind the desk was calling her name over and over snapping her back to reality. That day still haunted her. It was the last time she'd seen her brother, now it was time to face him.

"Mr. Duke will see you now!" Jon Jon exclaimed with a chipper spirit. Because she looked like she wasn't feeling well, he got up from his desk to help her up. Jon Jon knew who she was. What he didn't understand was why she was here now? What did she want from Duke? And lastly, was he gonna have to fuck her up? "Right through the mahogany door," he directed her.

Startisha was aware that she must have looked like a fool to that Jon Jon guy. However, thinking about that day at the reading of the will really had her in her feelings.

Pushing through the large door, she tried hard to blow her anxiety out with her next breath then walked through the door with practiced confidence. Sitting behind the large, white, lacquer desk was a man she admired more than she wanted to admit.

They had never spoken a word to each other, but he was a living symbol of the family she wanted so desperately.

"Well are you gonna stand there and look at me or are you gonna come in?" Duke was smiling on the inside at how vulnerable she always appeared to be.

Moving forward slowly but gracefully, Startisha shook off her anxiety. She needed to state her case, so it was either now or never. Looking around the office as she entered, the charm and elegance did not go unrecognized. The entire room was white lacquer with walnut tops. There was a large wet bar with glass racks. The three seat, pure white, leather sofa was to die for. All the white was accented with warm browns and golds. The 75" flat screen had the new cable fashion channel playing with the volume turned down.

She hadn't seen her brother in five years; she was thirteen then but now she was an adult and she needed him to consider her as such. She knew for a fact that he followed her career, there was no way he wasn't aware of what she was doing; it just wasn't in him. "Hello Hudson, thank you for seeing me." She had heard that he didn't like being called Hudson, but until he told her directly, she was gonna call him what their father called him.

Duke looked at her like she was crazy, he knew she was playing games, but he could play games as well. As he watched her take a seat in the high back leather chair, he thought to himself,

She better come correct, because I'm the best chess player she will ever meet, but I can show her better than I can tell her. "What can I do for you Startisha?" Duke's tone was all business.

Instantly, Startisha felt like a little girl in his presence, which was so different from how self-assured she was in her daily life. It was like Duke knew all of her insecurities. She hated how he made her feel, so she decided to use that fear.

Sitting up straight in the chair, she matched his nonchalant demeanor as she said, "I want my inheritance turned over to me. I need to use it to push my modeling career to the next level. I know you're gonna repeat what Poppa wanted for me, but it's not what I wanted." Pausing, she took a breath but kept right on talking. "Modeling has always been my dream. Poppa never took into account what I wanted, it's not fair." There, she had said it, and to the person she wanted to say it to. Her mother begged her not to do it, but Startisha refused to be hidden away any longer.

Duke studied his baby sister as she spoke. She was definitely sexy; she moved like a dancer and had a face like a beautiful dream. He could see his father as well as himself in her face and definitely in her attitude. Yet, her mere presence reminded him of the pain in his mother's eyes. He felt he owed his mother the respect of not forging a relationship with the bastard child of his father. Furthermore, he believed he owed it to his father to honor his last will and testament. Duke grabbed his temples with his hands, massaging them as he leaned back in his chair.

This is one reason why he didn't have a family of his own. He wasn't ready to make a mess like his parents did.

Taking a deep breath, he sat up in his chair and said to his anxiety-ridden sister. "When our father died, a part of me died with him. We were close and did a lot together, but he never told me about you." Duke got up from his chair, walked around, and sat on the edge of his desk, never breaking eye contact with his sister. "So imagine my surprise when you showed up at his funeral and announced to the world that you were his daughter. I knew you weren't lying, but you were young and unable to grasp the damage that your revelation would cause." Switching his weight on the desk, he folded his arms. Startisha attempted to speak but he raised his hands to stop her. "My mother had a stroke that day. I never found out why you and your mother were at the hospital. It was the one thing that never made sense to me. When I went toward your mother, she looked at me and ran away, and you ran behind her. It seems you guys are always running away."

Without warning, Duke stood, walked behind his desk, and sat back down. His demeanor was changing rapidly but he was trying very hard to maintain his composure. "My mother has never recovered from that horrible day five years ago. Her life was forever changed. I don't know what you expect of me, but you can forget it. My father's last will and testament will be followed to the letter. So if you want anything, I suggest you enroll in law school. Now if you don't mind, I have work to do." With that, Duke picked up the phone and told Jon Jon to get Bri on the phone.

Tapping the keys on his keyboard, he noticed Startisha hadn't moved. Duke never looked up but stated, "This is when you leave my office and my building."

Holding back tears, Startisha stood quickly from the chair. She refused to let him see her drop a tear, but she wasn't going to leave without cussing his arrogant ass out. "Fuck you H*U*D*S*O*N*! You can look down on me all you want, but eventually, you will have to deal with me! I am a DUKE too! You can't change that no matter how hard you try. It was not my intent for anything to happen to your mother, other than for her to know the truth. My mother and I felt bad, that's why we came to the hospital. I will NOT kiss your ass, but I will get what's owed to me!" She turned quickly and left the office before she jumped across the massive desk and choked the shit out of her big brother.

It wasn't until she made it to the lobby that Startisha finally allowed the tears to roll down her cheeks. She ran pass Jon Jon so fast she could hear him in the distance calling behind her. Doubled over and heaving, she stood in the lobby for what seemed like hours, thinking, *I have got to get myself together.* There was a tap on her shoulder that caused her to jump damn near out of her skin. "I'm sorry; I didn't mean to scare you. I was just checking to see if you were ok; I don't mean any harm."

Startisha straightened up and pressed her hands down her dress to make sure she was presentable before she turned to face the helpful stranger. When she turned around, there was a beautiful, white lady dressed in a fly Valentino business suit. "I'm fine, thank you very much." Startisha looked a little embarrassed.

Marta knew exactly who she was. Duke tried his best to keep her hidden, but here she was in the BM lobby crying like a baby. "Hey, aren't you Startisha Duke?" Marta made sure to sound excited and star struck.

It was obvious that Startisha was trying to find her way into the Duke family but still being shut out. Marta smiled at Startisha as the wheels in her mind turned, wondering how she could use her to destroy her brother.

A smile crept on Startisha's face. The mere fact that someone recognized her as a Duke and not that model girl was enough to make her glow internally. It was weird how important it was to her. Then again, she was now ready to say fuck it and show her big brother she could be just as coldhearted as he was. Making eye contact with the woman, she held her head high as she gave her a warm smile. "Yes, I am Startisha Duke. Who are you?" Startisha felt her confidence growing as she spoke.

The lobby was starting to get busy. Though the women passing through were extremely beautiful, none of them could really hold a candle to Startisha. To put it lightly, she was stunning. Marta could see a lot of Duke in her features.

Marta decided she would befriend her by playing to her ego and insecurities at the same time. Offering her hand to shake, she said, "I'm sorry, how rude of me. I'm Marta, Marta VanDyke, CFO of Glamour Girls. It's so nice to finally meet you Ms. Duke." Marta shook hands with the girl who she felt could turn things around.

Marta was running late for her meeting with Lance Duke but he could wait. Right now, she had to get in the head of the person who was the answer to all of her problems. Smiling warmly, she touched Startisha's arm lightly. "You know what? I think it would be an excellent idea to get to know you since our companies will be working closely together.

Do you have time to have lunch with me?" Marta asked, attempting as best she could to hide her deception. The smile that broke out on Startisha's face could have won her an academy award had she been in a movie. If there was one thing her mother taught her, it was how to spot a fake bitch and that's exactly what she had run into. Startisha didn't know what Marta's game was, but figured the best way to find out was to play along. Smiling to herself, Startisha thought, *Fucking with me she'll find out it ain't no fun when the rabbit's got the gun.*

Cheating In The Next Room

The resort city of Virginia Beach was a vacation destination for lovers. The clear blue water, clubs, restaurants, and numerous five star hotels drew tourists by the boatload. The Oceanside Resort Hotel was one of many. Pulling up to valet, Jason had to say he was impressed, he thought to himself, *At least this chick has taste.* His door opened and a man in a uniform bowed slightly then ushered him away from his Lexus after handing him a ticket. Jason offered the man a tip but he refused. He told Jason that his tip had already been taken care of by the lady. That revelation caused Jason to pause. He stood at the entrance of the hotel looking at each shoulder for those devils.

Sitting in the room waiting for Jason, she was a ball of nerves. Charmaine wanted everything to be perfect. She ordered strawberries and cheese from room service, checked the mood lighting in the room, and made sure the bar was fully stocked. As she walked pass the floor length mirror, Charmaine had to stop and take stock of herself. At 5'7", she wasn't too short nor too tall. In fact, most men thought she was just right.

Her body was well put together with 165 lbs. of thickness that was evenly distributed between her hips, thighs, and breasts. Gliding her hands over her body, the word that came to her mind was luscious. Charmaine wondered what Jason saw in Bri. From her perspective, she was prettier than Bri, and her body was tighter and thicker than Bri's. *So why is he with her instead of me?* Before she could answer her own question, there was a knock at the door. Charmaine took a deep breath and pushed her bra up to make sure she was sitting right.

Taking one last look, she made her way to the door, ready to claim her man.

Standing in front of the door, Jason put on his game face. He was ready to bitch slap whoever was on the other side of the door. It was hard enough being married. So when people intentionally interfered, it made happiness nearly impossible. Jason had been dealing with the Phantom now for over a year; therefore, he was ready to get to the bottom of it. Jason called Brent after the Phantom told him where to meet her, and he told him it wasn't a good idea. Brent laughed as he said

"Man, you don't even know who the hell you meeting. It could be some transsexual dude-chick ready to make a love connection. You better carry your ass on home and work it out with Bri."

Jason chuckled to himself as he remembered his best friend's advice. Nonetheless, there he stood waiting for the Phantom to open the door. Looking down the long corridor, Jason swore to himself that if a dude-chick opened the door, he was going to chop him in the jugular. Just as he had that thought, the door opened slowly. They both stood there staring at one another long enough for each of them to become uncomfortable. Jason couldn't believe it; it was Bri's secretary. Damn, he never remembered her looking like a boss chick before. From where he was standing, this chick, or Charmaine if he remembered correctly, was fucking banging and it didn't help that he hadn't had sex in days.

Charmaine cleared her throat. "I'm glad you came Jason, come in." Turning around, she gave him an eye full of her lusciousness.

There was no way Jason could miss the seduction as he walked further into the room, where there was mood lighting, light jazz playing, and even a covered tray from room service. Jason smiled at the fact that she went all out. It was difficult to imagine why she would put so much time and effort into another woman's husband; it just didn't make sense to him.

Charmaine moved into the plush seating area where she had a plate of cheese and crackers already set out. She planned on saving the strawberries for later. Her mind was spinning; it was hard to believe that he was actually in a hotel room with her and not just in her dreams. She needed to do everything right. It was her time with her man. After tonight, he would leave Bri and be with her only. The mere thought of the expression on Bri's face when Jason told her he was leaving her was enough to make her pussy drip. Turning around quickly, she caught Jason starring at her. "Come here Jason, sit down and let me feed you." Charmaine bent over, supposedly to pick up the tray, but she was really offering Jason something else to eat.

Despite his efforts, Jason couldn't stop his dick from rising at the sight of a naked, round ass. Yeah, that's right, naked ass. Charmaine answered the door in nothing but a bra, thong, and stilettos. The sight was beyond sexy with a mixture of slutty just like he liked it.

It was at that exact moment that the devil on his shoulder won the fight. Before she could make another move, Jason was parting her cheeks and moving her thong to the side. The sight of her pink lips dripping as they stared back at him drove him over the edge.

89

Jason released his monster from his pants; he could hear her panting as he rubbed his dick up and down her pulsating box, getting his dick nice and juicy. But he wasn't going to give her exactly what she wanted; he was going to take what he wanted. Charmaine was grinding her hips, trying to get him to fuck her. She wasn't prepared when he shoved his dick into her ass in one movement. She screamed slightly and tried to release herself from his grasp, but Jason began to slow grind while he played with her pussy, forcing her to submit to his desires.

"Yes Jason! Baby, don't stop; please don't stop...I love it!" Charmaine screamed her enjoyment as she met him pound for pound while thrusting her hips back to meet each thrust.

Watching her ass bounce up and down on his dick was causing the beast to come out of Jason. He split her open without regard, never saying a word. His left toe began to twitch, which was always a sign that he was nearing the end. Jason went extra hard as he thought about all the confusion this broad was trying to cause in his life. The harder he dug in her, the more she seemed to enjoy it. Strangely, that turned him on even more. Shaking his head, Jason tried not to enjoy it as much as he was. The guilt began to set in just as his body began to shake. He pulled out and bust across her back with some of his creamy goodness landing on the back of her hair.

Wiping the sweat from his eyes, Jason attempted to catch his breath. When he looked down at Charmaine, his treachery hit him full circle as he thought, *This crazy broad ain't never gonna leave me alone now. This was a dumb move.*

Jason attempted to put some distance between himself and Charmaine's glistening pussy. It was calling him and he needed to think clearly.

Charmaine smiled inside as she watched Jason have his private battle. She knew it would be hard for him to resist her after he had a shot of ass. Pulling herself together, she went to the bar to make him a drink. Hennessey and Coke with a twist of lime and no rocks; don't ask how she knew exactly how he took his drink, but she did. In fact, there was a lot about Jason that she knew as he would soon find out. "Here you go baby, drink this." Charmaine handed him his drink then turned and left without saying another word.

The bounce in her ass was mesmerizing. All he could think was, *left cheek, right cheek;* it was like a hypnotic dance and he was caught in the trance. Jason didn't normally allow his mind to be persuaded by the booty, but the lack of pussy makes for strange bed fellows. Sipping on his drink, he pushed the glass away and stared at it for a second then looked toward the door that Charmaine went into.

All the while thinking to himself, *this chick is up to some shit. She put that ass on me real proper. Plus, she knows how to make my drink. If I didn't know any better, I would say she trynna make a nigga keep fucking with her.*

Deciding he needed to set her straight, Jason downed the rest of his drink then headed to holla at Charmaine. The steam of the shower made a sexy silhouette of her thickness.

She lathered herself with her favorite fragrances as she dreamed about Jason rubbing his hands all over her body.

Her daydream was about him actually loving her the way he loved Bri. She wanted him to cherish her; yeah, that's what she was missing. She was confident she could get him to fuck her, but could she get him to want her like he wanted water or air? This was where Charmaine always had a problem. Men loved fucking her, but none of them stayed around to love her. Tears slowly flowed down her face as she rubbed her breasts, wishing she knew what it was about her that made men overlook her. There was a slight breeze that caused her to look over her shoulder.

She was so into her sorrow and confusion that she never heard Jason enter the shower. Her insides were jumping. Charmaine wasn't used to being this emotional. Reaching out, he wiped her tears away, pulled her into his arms, and let the water cover them both as he whispered in her ear.

"What's going on with you? Why are you in here crying like this?" Jason wasn't even sure why he cared. He just didn't like to see women cry, or was it that she was getting to him some kind of way? He just didn't understand why he was moving like he was.

Being held felt amazing, it had to be at the top of the most romantic things to do list. Charmaine felt safe in Jason's arms. Hearing him sound concerned about her was more than she could have ever hoped for. Charmaine reached down and stroked his thickness until her hand could no longer handle it.

The mosaic tile was a sexy shade of burnt orange and brown, but right now, Charmaine's back was adding to the custom design as Jason pushed her body against the tile and entered her with one massive thrust. Closing her legs around his girth, Charmaine started a slow grind, but Jason had something else in mind.

With one of her breasts in his mouth, he bottomed out on Charmaine's ass and pounded her relentlessly. Jason was holding on to her hips, moving mercilessly to an imaginary beat that only he could hear. The water was beating down his back, adding to the sensation.

In ecstasy, Charmaine was damn near screaming; she had lost count of how many times she had cum. Tightening the muscles in her love box and matching Jason stroke for stroke, her only concern, at the moment, was to ensure that she became his favorite ride.

The scene had to look like something out of a sexy erotica movie–steam covered every crevice in the large ensuite bathroom, two naked bodies silhouetted through the shower door, a fuck session so strong that both parties were in need of a drink and a nap, in that order. Jason could feel that infamous tingling in his toes and knew it was almost time for the monster to erupt. He sucked on Charmaine's neck, breathing hard, and thinking to himself, *Damn, this some good ass pussy. Fuck, she taking this dick too.* With that last thought, he lifted Charmaine off of him and pushed her to her knees.

He didn't even have to instruct her, she immediately took his dick in her mouth, and let the volcano erupt down her throat. Jason watched her in awe, it was just that sexy.

By the time he woke up, it was 11 p.m. Jason felt like he had a hangover. While adjusting his eyes to the room, his memory started coming back to him. Turning his head to the right, his eyes rested on the plump ass tooted toward him. Deep inside, he knew he was wrong. Hell, this was exactly what he was trying to prevent in his own marriage, but this is the type of shit that happens when you play hide the pussy at home.

When wives play games, another bitch will step up and offer him a full buffet. Jason got up slowly, heading to the shower. There was no need to go home soaked in another woman's juices. He let the hot water run over his head and down his back as his mind tried to wrap around the complications he had just added to his already complex situation. Jason loved his wife, he didn't doubt that.

On the other hand, he was also aware that they had serious problems in their marriage. It was time to address their issues and stop creating new ones.

Charmaine was sitting up in bed plotting when Jason walked back in fully dressed. She was hoping he would stay the night, but she understood that he had to get back home and let Bri know shit was about to change. She had butterflies as their eyes met.

In his eyes, all she could detect was lust and happiness; she watched as he licked his lips, which damn near made her wet the sheets. Before she could say anything, he spoke up.

"Charmaine, what we did today was fucked up, it was wrong. You caught me at a time when I'm going through something with Bri and I let that fuck my decision making up. You wanted some dick, you got some dick."

He paused to let what he said sink in. If the pissed off look on her face was any indication, Jason could see that he was getting through to her, so he continued. "Fact is, I love my wife, and giving me a shot of ass will not change that. Do you understand what I'm saying?"

Seeing red, Charmaine jumped up from the bed and rushed Jason, swinging her fist while her titties bounced from right to left. The sight would have been hilarious if it wasn't so sexy. She landed a punch to his ear before he could block her then he grabbed her arms, pinning them behind her back.

"Fuck is wrong with you girl. You acting like you didn't know I was a married man, fuck is yo problem?" Jason was struggling to hold on as she kicked and struggled in his grasp.

"Urrrrrrrgh! I hate you fucking niggas, man! Y'all always playing with a bitch like me, but not this time. This time, you gon' pay the piper." Suddenly, Charmaine stopped struggling and a calm came over her.

Inside, she felt something break, not something as cliché as her heart. She actually felt like she was becoming unglued.

Her breathing was even now; but her mind was moving a mile a minute as she said barely above a whisper, "Tell you what you're gonna do…you're gonna go home to your WIFE!" She jerked her arms out of his grasp before she continued then turned to face Jason with red eyes, refusing to shed the tears that were threatening to fall. "I will give you a week to figure out how you come back to me. After that, shit's gonna get real."

Charmaine didn't even wait for Jason to respond before she turned and walked away. The last thing Jason heard as he stood there watching her cheeks move from left to right was the slamming of the bathroom door. Shaking his head, he grabbed his wallet and cell phone and headed toward the door, thinking to himself, *Bitches is crazy.* He turned his phone back on and his notifications immediately went off. Seeing that it was a little after 11:45 p.m., Jason already knew it was Bri.

At least he hoped it was Bri checking up on him. Pushing the elevator button to head to the lobby, he opened his text message icon.

With a slight smirk, he thought to himself, *Maybe wondering where I am will make her get some act right.* Next, he read the first text message twice just to make sure it said what he thought it said.

10 p.m.: If you ain't dead STAY THE FUCK WHERE YOU AT!

Home Alone

After much soul searching, Bri decided she needed to talk to her husband. The ghost of her childhood would probably haunt her for the rest of her life. Nevertheless, now it was time to face her demons. At least that's how she felt when she left the office. Now that she was relaxing at home, she wasn't quite sure. It was difficult for her to explain her feelings, which is why she usually didn't. Briann Jennings did exactly what she wanted to do, plain and simple. Any man who wanted to be in her world was just gonna have to learn to cope with it.

Bri relaxed on her comfortable chaise lounge for hours as she tried to make sense of her life. So many thoughts were going through her mind, all of which came back to, *Why did I get married?* The question almost startled her, but it was a damn good question. Briann never planned on getting married; she never planned to turn her life over to a man like her mother did. Jason broke down defenses in her that she wasn't even consciously aware of. Looking at the clock, it read 9:55 p.m. Bri yawned, not even realizing it was that late. She didn't recall hearing Jason come in.

Getting up from the couch, she made her way up the spiral staircase with plans of making love to her husband. Sex was the great equalizer; her plan was to put that good shit on him then lie in his arms and talk until they came to an arrangement that worked for both of them. Bri didn't think she could fully consent to what Jason was asking, but she did understand his point of view which was half the battle. When she entered their bedroom, it was just as quiet as the rest of the house.

Going into the ensuite, she found it empty as well. Bri pushed the button on the security system to view the garage and the circular driveway only to see Jason's car wasn't there. At this point, Bri was seeing red. *See, this the bullshit I be talking about, I'm not gon' go through it, not me,* she thought to herself. Picking up her cell phone, she sent him a text, dropped it on her bed then headed to the shower. She refused to be played, especially by her husband.

Thirty minutes later, she was pulling her shiny new GSF Lexus out of her driveway. With her brain moving a mile a minute, she pushed the 467-horsepower to the limit; she had to get away. Bri cursed herself for getting caught up.

She didn't want to be where Jason was or even where he wasn't; she refused to let her nerves be plucked. Shaking her head as she weaved through the streets, she started talking to herself, which was something she said she would never do, particularly behind a man. "This nigga got me all kinds of fucked up. He has no clue that I let him be the exception to MY rule, when I should have just fucked him and let his ass be. Now he's trynna play me like monopoly, nah…you can't play a bitch who owns Boardwalk nigga." Slowing down, she tried to let her body relax and sink into the high back sport seat. This was only the second time she had driven the Lexus, she inhaled the new car smell and smirked, "Boardwalk and Park Place Bitch."

French inspired sophistication surrounded the gated, golf course community of Broadmure. The neighborhood was beyond elegant and Bri knew elegance.

She recalled considering this part of town when she was looking for a home. There was a certain original charm and history to the area that caught her eye. Pulling up to the six foot wrought iron gate, Bri began having second thoughts. Shaking her head, she put her hand out the window and pushed the call button on the security wall.

This is not the time to second-guess myself, she thought. There was a slight crackle from the speaker.

"Briann, what are you doing here?" The deep baritone voice came through the speaker loud and clear.

Bri tried not to laugh because he sounded so unsure of himself, which was so unlike him. Instead, she looked at the monitor and winked as she said, "Open the gate and you will surely find out, that is if you're not scared." Before she could finish, the gate began to slowly open. Bri pulled forward with a knowing twinkle in her eye, thinking to herself, *Duke is far from stupid, he know he wants this pussy.*

"Briann better stop playing with me." Duke said out loud as he made his way up from his man cave to let her in. He lived alone in nine thousand square feet of luxury. With five bedrooms and four and a half baths, he was the ultimate bachelor. Duke dated the who's who of women, all with the right amount of sexy, class, and pedigree. What he couldn't find was a woman that made him hold his breath.

That is, until he met Briann. Wearing only his Calvin Klein pajama bottoms, Duke opened his door just as Briann was about to knock.

"So what do I owe this very special delivery?" The words drifted from Duke's mouth, attempting to hide the lust that was behind every word.

Bri was in awe of the fantasy that stood before her. She knew Duke was fine, but who knew he was FIONE! The way his chest shined from the porch light only highlighted the tightness of his triceps, biceps, and oh gawd, his chest. It was like her eyes had a mind of their own as they traveled from his chest down to the elastic of his pajama bottoms. It was the cough from Duke that stopped her from gawking. "Well do I have to show you out here on the porch or do you plan on inviting me in?" Bri recovered quickly as she slithered pass Duke and entered his space.

Neither of them noticed the headlights that passed by the security gate at that moment. Duke was more focused on the firestorm that had just invaded his home.

All he could do was shake his head as he admired the full-length, midnight blue, fur and stilettos, wondering what event she was coming from that caused her to get all jazzy, while mentally checking his calendar. He closed his door, being sure to lock it and set the alarm.

Turning back to face Bri, Duke stopped in his tracks, while allowing his eyes to roam over pure perfection. Although he had imagined it in his dreams a million times, at that very moment, he could only stare in amazement.

While Duke messed around with the alarm, Bri was getting ready to set shit off. Dropping her full length fur to the rug below, she posed seductively, ensuring that all of her assets were on display. Jason wasn't gonna be the only one fucking tonight; Bri was determined to break Duke in properly. When he turned around, all she saw in his eyes was lust and desire. Inwardly, she smiled as he took in every inch of her curves. For a minute, she thought he was gonna stare all day. Finally, he started walking slowly in her direction, causing pussy muscles to twitch. Simply watching him move was like a melody; he was smooth and strong at the same damn time.

Most of all, he was fucking sexy and Bri wanted him right then. It wasn't until Duke stopped in front of her and licked his lips did he make a sound. Actually, what he did was whisper in her ear. Whatever he said caused a sensuous reaction in Bri.

Without hesitation, she bent down, pulling his pajama pants as she went. Her eyes grew large with appreciation when she noticed the nice thick package he was carrying. It was just like she envisioned, but nothing compared to being saluted in person. A moan escaped her throat just as she took him in her mouth. The juices that escaped coated his dick while she tightened the suction and showed him why she was the showstopper.

"Shhhhhhhhit! Oh fuck Briann, suck this dick baby." Duke couldn't stop his chant as he stood his ground, watching Bri's performance of what had to be the best fellatio ever.

He wasn't sure if she was normally this good or if him whispering in her ear that he was going to fuck the shit out of her until the cops came knocking caused her to suck his dick with so much gusto. Regardless of her reasons, he gave her a gold star, a Grammy, an Oscar, and a damn Super Bowl ring for her performance.

The veins in his thickness were increasing to the point that Bri felt they would pop. She increased her rhythm as the waterfall in her mouth caused his knees to buckle.

Bri couldn't believe she finally had the sexy Duke in her web; she was determined to make him a part of her weekly routine. Before she could ponder her plans any longer, Duke pulled her up from her knees then picked her up as if she weighed absolutely nothing. She closed her legs around his waist just as he inserted his monster inside. Holding onto his thick shoulders, she leaned back while Duke plowed deep into her womanhood.

The sounds coming from Bri was all the encouragement Duke needed to go harder. She was begging him not to stop, which only made him turn it up a notch. Thinking about the things he wanted to do to her caused him to go into overdrive. He could feel her insides contracting on his dick. Bri was well into her third nut as the wetness cascaded down his shaft, causing him to lose it.

Duke felt himself nearing the end, grabbing Bri's ass cheeks with both hands; he lifted her up and down on his dick at a rapid pace.

He loved how she met the challenge with abandon, screaming for him to fuck her; and that's exactly what he did.

"Shit Briann, I'm 'bout to bust baby. Keep fucking me just like that shitttttt. Here it comes baby…urrrrrrrrrrghhhhhhhhhhhhhhhhh!" Duke released his pent-up lust into Bri. As his breathing regulated, he licked her neck and ears. He loved the way she continued to grind on his dick, causing his manhood to prepare for round two. Still holding him tightly around the neck, Duke walked with Bri to his bedroom for rounds two, three, and if she could hang, round four.

Dirty
After spending all day with Startisha, Marta drove to
Bri's neighborhood. There was no game plan, her car just
acted as if it had a mind of its own. Maybe her vehicle
knew how to deal with the internal turmoil better than
she did. Staring straight ahead, Marta felt so unsure of
herself. Should she knock on Bri's door and confront her
with how she felt or should she sit back and wait for her
to come to her willingly. Marta knew Bri wasn't the type
of woman you could give an ultimatum to. Bri needed to
see for herself that Marta was the only person who really
had her best interest at heart. Deciding that's what she
would do, Marta started her car prepared to go home.
Before she could pull off, the five car garage door opened
and a midnight blue Lexus came speeding out and
through the circular driveway. Marta caught a glimpse of
Bri as she sped by. Going home was forgotten.
Determined to see where she was going, Marta sped off
behind Bri.

Marta followed Bri into a posh neighborhood, thinking
maybe she had an event to go to that wasn't on the
Glamour Girls calendar. It would be just like Bri to show
up to an event well past fashionably late.

Smiling at the thought, Marta watched Bri push the
button at the security gate. Once Bri entered, Marta drove
by slowly, noticing there were no other vehicles around.
Backing her car up, Marta watched as Bri knocked on the
door. When the door opened and Duke's shirtless frame
filled the doorway, Marta could feel her blood pressure
spike.

Pissed, she sat in her car outside of Duke's mansion. That
was the best way she could describe her emotional state.

The very thing she wanted to prevent had come to pass. Now Marta had to move her game plan into overdrive, thinking out loud, she said, "Enjoy her while you can, but if I can't have her, none of y'all will." The flowing tears were unrecognizable even to Marta as she sped out of the pricey neighborhood. At this point, she was ready to do Bri dirty.

Family Matter

Startisha had a lot of thinking to do after spending the entire afternoon with Marta. Never attempting to hide her contempt, she listened to Marta go on and on about Bri and Duke. If it wasn't so real, it would be hilarious. Startisha wondered where all of the distain was coming from. If she didn't know any better, she would think Marta was jealous but of what. Was she interested in Duke, was that it? Or was she, god forbid, interested in Bri? Whatever it was, she had herself all worked up. Surfing the web, Startisha ended up on Glamour Girls' website. She read up on the company's history, products, and the owner herself. It was amazing to see a African American woman fulfill the goals she set out to accomplish. Smiling as she continued to read, Startisha could only admire Bri and that got her to thinking.

The clanking of keys alerted her to Jakari's arrival, checking the hidden camera she smiled. The blush that enveloped her cheeks was real. Jakari was her peace, her heart, and the one person other than her mother who supported her wholeheartedly.

"Star…Star…where ya at mama?" Jakari yelled in what sounded to her like a smooth R&B song.

She loved the way he made her feel; he was her family. Jakari was just what she needed to combat her deep-rooted issues. Checking out her appearance in the reflection of the computer screen, Startisha smiled like a school girl; actually, that's where they met. Jakari and Startisha had been by each other's side since they were six years old, glued at the hip.

Her mother babysat him because both his parents worked two jobs in an effort to make ends meet. But Glenda never had to make ends meet, Poppa Duke saw to that. Poppa Duke paid her mortgage, brought clothes, paid for private lessons for Startisha–everything she needed. Well everything except acceptance. And that's where Jakari came in, he accepted her for who she was and made her feel wanted as well as needed. Staring at her reflection, a sadness washed over her as she remembered when she almost lost him.

Jakari was an only child, and at fifteen, he was having a really hard time fitting in. It was strange because he was an extremely handsome boy and all the girls liked him. That was until they realized he wasn't down.

He followed the rules, did what his parents told him to do and was a good student. Jakari was what the kids called a computer geek and a damn good one at that.

Unfortunately, those qualities didn't work out too good for him. Instead, it made Jakari unsure of himself, and that's where Startisha played a huge role in his life. For the most part, she was as much his lifeline as he was hers. The boys in the neighborhood didn't see love and commitment. They saw what they called a pussy whipped nigga. At fifteen, Jakari let the boys get to him. When they joked that he couldn't hang out with them because Startisha would kick his ass, he went against his better judgment, got geared up, and snuck out of the house to hang with the neighborhood boys.

Jakari didn't make it back home for three years. The particulars of what happened were never fully explained. The only thing Startisha knew was someone got killed and somehow Jakari was one of the boys involved. Jakari was the youngest boy involved so he went through the juvenile court system, but the other seven boys were all over sixteen and could be tried as adults. Startisha and Jakari were once again each other's lifeline.

She rolled with him the entire time he was locked up; she wrote him, accepted his phone calls, and encouraged him. He listened to her dreams and insecurities but most of all, he motivated her to be who she was, a Duke.

"There you go baby, why you up here staring at a blank computer screen?" Jakari laughed as he kissed Startisha on the neck.

She couldn't help but smile deep inside. Jakari had only been home six months and just the smell of him was everything to her. Before she answered, she inhaled his masculinity and smiled. "You know Kari, I was just sitting here thinking how happy I am, and you do that for me. Oh, I was also thinking about how good you smell." They both burst out laughing at her revelation.

Getting up from the desk wearing no bra under his wife beater, her nipples were sitting at attention. The pink, ruffled boy shorts crept slightly between her cheeks. Startisha went to fix her boy shorts until she heard, "Leave 'em. Matter fact, let me see those cheeks move for me baby." Jakari was leaning on the desk watching his woman give the sexiest stripper dance ever.

He had really grown up in the three years that he was away. No longer did he give a fuck about what anybody had to say about his relationship with his baby. Not following his heart or using his head had already cost him so much.

The entire time he was locked up, the only voice that got through his shield was Startisha. The only one that got through the block in his heart was Startisha. And despite other chicks trying to throw pussy at him left and right, Startisha was the only woman he had ever been with. Watching her right now was causing his heart to swell in his chest. When he was released from prison, Startisha had been living in her own house for about seven months. She wrote him about it, excited that she could make a home for them and that's exactly what she had been doing. Between her modeling assignments and trying to get recognized on a larger scale, she had been holding him down. In his head, Jakari could hear that Lil Ronny joint *left cheek, right cheek* he had to shake it off before he got sidetracked.

"Come here Star." Jakari smacked her on her ass as he pulled her up. Jakari loved looking into her smiling face, it calmed him.

One thing he knew for sure was it was his turn to hold her down. Only he knew the one thing she wanted more than anything. If it was the last thing he did, he planned to give it to her. Jakari pulled her close to him and gave her the deepest kiss he could.

The kiss was a thank you; it was I love you; it was a, you are my everything kiss. When he pulled back, he could see the tears flowing down his Star's face. Jakari kissed her eyes before he wiped her tears with his thumb. Cradling her face in his hands he said, "I got an IT job today baby." He had such a serious look on his face.

Startisha closed herself in his arms so quickly, he almost lost his balance. She was screaming and crying at the same time, saying, "Whoot! Whoot! Whoot! I'm so proud of you baby. Tell me everything, where is it at, tell me baby!" Startisha was so excited for her man. She knew how super-talented and passionate he was about computers and technology.

There was no denying that his woman had his best interest at heart. He loved her for that. Now it was time to help her get what she wanted. Gazing deep into her eyes, he said, "You are looking at the new IT Tech Specialist for Beauty Mark, Inc."

That's What Friends Are For
After reading the text from Bri over again and again, Jason decided going home probably wasn't such a good idea. As he drove past the exit to his neighborhood for the second time, he just kept driving. It wasn't that he was scared of Bri; shit, he was the man of his home. "Besides, some of this is her own damn fault," he reasoned out loud. Jason felt that Bri's behavior pushed him to do what he did. It was easy to blame her, but harder to take a look at the real problem. Jason looked at himself in the rear view mirror and could admit that he wasn't happy with what he saw. What he needed was some sound advice from someone who was on track with their shit. He didn't need to talk to a nigga that was still running the street fucking six bitches and running from four baby mommas. It was no surprise when he found himself pulling into the driveway of his best friend in the world.

There was that noise again, it sounded like his phone vibrating on the floor. Brent could have sworn he left that thing downstairs.

With one eye open and his head still in a fog, he reached over the side of the bed, moving his hand around, searching for the phone.

He was trying his best not to wake Sonya. If he woke her, she was going to be pissed and Brent didn't want to deal with that fury. Running behind the triplets all day and studying for the bar exam at night, sleep was a precious commodity in the Warner household. The phone buzzed again just as he touched it on the floor.

Answering as quietly as possible, Brent slowly rose from the bed after he saw who it was. "Jay, what the hell you doing calling me so late; what happened?" Brent said now fully awake and walking across the plush carpet gently.

Jason was standing on Brent's porch trying to look normal, like it wasn't strange for him to be standing there at 12:30 in the morning. Looking around the cookie cutter neighborhood, Jason envied Brent's life. His friend had it all, a regular marriage, three healthy and happy kids, and a career he loved. Hearing his sleepy friend finally answer the phone, Jason felt a little guilty. "I'm so sorry B, I'm at your front door man, come let me in." Jason felt bad about intruding, but that's what friends are for.

The door opened before Jason could get too sentimental. He made a move to walk into the house when he heard,

"Jason Matthews! What the hell you doing here waking up my damn household?" Sonya raised her voice in frustration. Jason shook his head back and forth as he walked into the house and closed the door. He sure didn't mean to wake Sonya's evil ass up. He already knew that wasn't going to be good. Looking around the living room, Jason saw Brent's ass standing near the mantel as if his wife wasn't screaming on him. The smirk on Brent's face didn't go unnoticed by Jason. Sonya wasn't done fussing. She was hollering about having to be up early with the kids, changing pampers, fixing bottles, and cleaning house. If he didn't feel bad before, he felt like an ass at that moment.

"Okay! Okay! Okay! Sonya gon' carry your sexy ass back to bed and get yo beauty rest. Let me talk to Jason." Brent gave her a hug and kissed her forehead saying, "Get some sleep baby; I'll be up in a bit."

Sonya gave Jason one more evil look before she headed back up the steep steps stomping hard. Jason could only laugh at Sonya's antics; they had a love-hate relationship. She was aware of his lifestyle and wasn't shy about showing her disapproval.

He knew she thought he was trying to pull Brent into some freaky shit, but it couldn't be further from the truth. Jason would never put a monkey wrench in his best friend's relationship like that. He was the unofficial godfather to the triplets and he took that shit serious. On the low, he was hurt that Sonya wouldn't let him be the official godfather, but not even that would make him disrespect her marriage to his boy. Jason watched her hips sway as she stomped and just shook his head before he heard Brent clear his throat.

"Jay, what the hell did you do? I mean you did something 'cause you look like shit. What's up?" Brent rambled off the questions as he walked into the kitchen to get a couple of cokes. He felt he was gonna need the caffeine to deal with whatever foolishness his boy was about to drop on him.

The look on Jason's face was like a kid who had just got caught with his hands in the cookie jar. In reality, that's exactly what was happening. Brent had already warned him not to meet the Phantom, but he wouldn't listen. Now, an already complicated issue between him and Bri was even more complicated.

Following Brent out of the kitchen, Jason came clean. "Man B, I should have listened to you."

Jason was shaking his head back and forth as he sat down on the comfortable couch. He noticed how clean the area was. If you didn't know any better, you would never think that three infants were in the home. He noticed Brent was staring at him, waiting for him to finish his thought, so he continued. "I went to meet the Phantom at the hotel." Raising his hand at the excited look in Brent's eye, he continued. "Now before you talk shit, wait until you hear who the hell it was." Jason was wringing his hands together. "I swear I was going there to fuck somebody up but when she answered the door, I don't know where my train of thought went. It was Charmaine, Bri's personal secretary." Jason threw his hands in the air to emphasize what he was saying.

Brent knew who Charmaine was. She was that sexy little number who flirted with him at the last party he went to at Glamour Girls even though she knew he was there with his wife. He didn't like her and wasn't at all surprised that she was the one sending the messages to Jason. "I don't trust that bitch. Please tell me you got the hell out of there Jay; please tell me that."

There was almost a pleading look on Brent's face, but as soon as he looked into his friends eyes, he knew shit went sideways. He sat back on the couch and crossed one leg over the other as he listened to Jason recount his evening shenanigans.

It wasn't until he mentioned the text message he got from Bri that Brent realized how deep this had really gotten. He knew how much Jason wanted his marriage to work.

Trying to be the optimistic friend, Brent told Jason to go to the guest room to sleep on it and look at the situation after he had some rest. Standing up, he said one last thing. "This thing with Charmaine has to stop now. If not, you will lose everything you've worked to achieve with Bri. You wanted this remember? That's what you told me, unless you've changed your mind."

Shaking his head, he left his best friend sitting on the couch looking stupid. He knew Jason was looking for some good insight from him, but he told him not to go to the hotel in the first damn place. Brent was kind of pissed as he headed upstairs to lie down with his wife.

Jason knew when Brent was mad. They went back too far and had been through way too much together to be able to hide how they felt.

Making his way into the purple and cream guest room, Jason sat down on the bed with a heavy heart. Brent was right though, after getting some rest he should be able to think with a clear mind. He had to get Charmaine to back off because he had no plans on leaving his wife. The softness of the pillow was a stark contrast to the head that melted into it. However, the softness had the effect that it was made for. Jason closed his eyes and before he could get comfortable, he was already asleep.

The Wrong Bitch

Charmaine was sitting at her desk, pissed. It had been two days since she had heard from Jason. To make matters worse, Bri had been away from the office for those two days as well. She communicated with Charmaine by phone, but refused to say where she was. Charmaine checked both of their social media accounts but there were no posts, tweets, or pics on the gram. She sent Jason at least ten inboxes and as many text messages but he never replied. The shit was about to make her go postal. Her mind was playing out the most disturbing scenarios. She could see Jason and Bri in a huge, luxury hotel room feeding each other strawberries with whip cream. Charmaine sent Bri a text telling her they needed to talk. She was going to get her man and that was that. Bri would just have to understand because she was definitely not prepared for the bitch that was coming to stake her claim.

A Breather

Bri hadn't been home in two days. Both her and Duke ran their perspective businesses from the comfort of his massive home office, well that was between sessions of sweet, sticky sex. No one knew where she was and that's just how she wanted it. Technology was such that you never really had to step foot into a brick and mortar office. There was only two days left before Glamour Girls would go to New York City to present its cosmetic catalog to the fashion week board. Bri still needed to review Glamour Girls cosmetic selections and the items that Beauty Mark wanted to add to the catalog. Furthermore, she wanted to review this year's theme that her marketing department had come up with and make some solid decisions today. Duke talked to his assistant, Jon Jon, about his computer upgrade while going through the marketing prospectus that Bri had handed him. Jason called her phone and texted non-stop on the first day. After reading a couple of the texts and listening to a couple of messages, Bri was even more confused as to what she wanted than ever. The text that she had gotten this morning had her in her feelings. Picking up her phone, she re-read Jason's text message again.

8:00 a.m. **So I guess you not answering me, calling me back, or even sending me a text is your way of saying it's over. Wow Bri! I want us to stop fucking other people and be a regular husband and wife, have some kids and grow old together, and that pushed you away like this? Then what the fuck did you get married for.**

I'm far from the bitch nigga whose gonna keep rolling with this bullshit so I tell you what. Take that nigga's dick out ya mouth and bring your ass home or your home will be empty when you decide to bring your ass to it.

"How many times have you read that text?" Duke kissed her neck causing her to blush.

Feeling a little embarrassed, Bri tried to put the phone back in her purse quickly but Duke grabbed her hand before she was able to put it away. "Look Briann, I never asked you what was going on between you and your husband and maybe I should have. I've tried to avoid this exact situation, but seeing you on my porch two nights ago was more than any man could take.

We can stay held up in here as long as you need to work out what's going on between you and him, but if you need to go to him baby, go." Duke attempted a smile.

Bri could see the hurt in Duke's eyes. He would never say it, but she could see it. It was never her plan to hurt anyone. She was too busy trying to deal with her own hurt and confused feelings. However, no matter what she tried to do, shit was just going to be messed up. Her cell phone notification buzzed and Bri reluctantly looked at the message. A frown appeared on her face as she read the text from Charmaine as she thought, *This chick oversteps her boundaries at times. It's time we had a sit down.*

Getting up from her seat, she followed Duke back into the ensuite bathroom. Watching him in the steam with his shoulders pressed up against the tile was making her knees shake. The water was streaming down his back; you could see it ripple through the steam. The scene was oh too sexy, but depressing as well for Bri. She had a lot of demons from her childhood chasing her and those same demons were playing a huge role in the decisions she was making.

Backing slowly out of the bathroom, Bri moved around the room quickly gathering her coat and purse. She stood in the middle of the room silently realizing that she didn't come with any clothes and shook her head in amazement at herself. It was time for her to deal with her life and either shit or get off the pot.

Duke heard the front door slam just as he got out of the shower. He figured Bri would be gone when he got finished. Walking through his bedroom, the first thing that caught his eye were the wrinkled sheets. *What have I gotten myself into? This woman is the only woman that's inside my head. Now that I've had her, I don't want anybody else to have her.* He thought as he slammed his hands together, Duke cursed himself for crossing that bridge. Now he was feeling a little loss. Grabbing clothes from his drawer, Duke began to get dressed. He needed to work on some of the numbers for the merger and the upcoming promotion for fashion season. He knew diving into work would take his mind off of his love life, or lack thereof. Dragging himself down the hall to his huge home office, Duke logged on to his computer.

The first email he opened didn't have a subject line. As he read the email, he could feel himself about to blow a fuse.

You have done everything to deny Startisha Duke her rightful place as a Duke. That stops today. This will be your only warning before I burn the Duke Empire to the ground.

There was no signature, just the cryptic message. Slamming his hand on the desk, he cursed out loud. Duke felt justified in shitting on Startisha but was aware that the public wouldn't see it that way. In his business, a good public image was important. Picking up the phone, he dialed the most important number in his rolodex.

"Hey, what you need?" The mysterious voice asked on the other end of the phone.

Clearing his throat in a hesitant manner, Duke said, "Its time." Then he hung up the phone and got up from his seat, walking solemnly over to the large picture window. The sun had finally set; it looked beautiful. Duke looked into the sky and talked to his father. "I'm sorry Poppa. I tried."

Jakari's Plan
In the two days that he had been at Beauty Mark, Jakari had yet to see the big man himself. There were rumors around the office about a big merger. Everyone was hopping around getting things in order. He was summoned to meet with Jon Jon, Duke's personal assistant. His IT team had already forewarned him that Jon Jon loved to hit on the help. What they didn't know was Startisha had already given him the rundown on the dude. She wasn't aware of his wild ways around the office, but she knew just from watching him during her last visit to Beauty Mark, that he was susceptible to manipulation from someone as sexy as Jakari. When his baby told him about Jon Jon, he began formulating a plan; now it was time to put it in place.

Walking into the penthouse suite, Jakari laughed to himself. He recalled Startisha telling him how underwhelmed she was with it. Shaking his head, he didn't quite see what all the fuss was about.

The décor was cool and it appeared to have everything that was needed in a lobby/reception area, including the cliché gay personal assistant. "Umm hello, are you Jon Jon?" Jakari asked as he stood in the doorway.

Jon Jon was tapping keys when he was interrupted by the sexiest man he had ever seen. He had heard from the other secretaries that the new man was pure eye candy but their descriptions didn't do him justice. Coming from around the desk, never losing eye contact with Mr. Melt in ya mouth, Jon Jon extended his hand.

"Hello, I'm Jon Jon and you must be our new IT genius." It wasn't what Jon Jon said it was definitely how he said it. His tone was dripping with lustful intentions.

Jakari tried his best not to throw up by extending his hand to greet the dude. He wore a sexy smirk as he said, "Yes, I am Jakari, not so sure about the genius, but I aim to please. Why don't you point me in the direction of the computer that needs my attention."

Jon Jon was wearing a pair of skintight, blue and white, pinstripe slacks and a sheer, white blouse. He switched past Jakari, hoping to tempt his tummy to the taste of milk and honey.

He wasn't quite sure if it worked, but a man could dream. "Ok Jakari, Duke needs a full refresh and all of his personal and company files backed-up and stored.

Next week, we will start the entire building on a refresh but the boss gets his first." Jon Jon explained as they walked toward Duke's desk.

The first thing Jakari noticed when he entered Duke's office was the large, white desk. He thought that shit was boss. In fact, the whole office was dope, from the 75 inch television to the white, leather sofas. Moving over to the desk, Jakari was in awe of the Apple G5 that Duke had set up. Blowing out a whistle, his mouth was salivating over working with the 16GB RAM; that shit was worth $10,000 by itself. Clapping his hands together, he looked toward Jon Jon and said, "Ok, I'm gonna get to work, shouldn't take me no more than two to three hours." He winked at Jon Jon before he sat down to get to work.

Jakari almost laughed as he watched Jon Jon practically skip out of the office on cloud nine as he thought to himself, *Let me get what I came for and get the fuck out of this company before I have to kill this dude.*

Jakari plugged his USB drive into Duke's computer and began to transfer all of his files from his hard drive.

Before he finished, he logged on to an external drive and sent Duke an email. Grabbing all of his equipment, Jakari was feeling really good. He hadn't felt this way since he came home. If he could put a word to it, he would say he felt useful, like he was doing something to finally help his baby. He was determined to find a way for Startisha to take her rightful seat as head of the Duke Family.

A Change Is Gonna Come

The plan was simple, Marta didn't plan on outwardly acting like a lovesick school girl; she had too much pride for that. Her plan was to hit Bri in her heart and take away the only thing that really mattered to her; Glamour Girls. She had put a lot of blood, sweat, and tears into the company, so she didn't want to destroy it. Currently, she felt underappreciated and outright disrespected. The fact that Bri was taunting her by parading Duke in her face was the straw that broke the camel's back. The door to the conference room opened and in walked Lance Duke, just like his cousin, he was ruggedly sexy. For Marta, Lance represented everything she hated at that moment. Nevertheless, she needed him to put her plan into action.

"Hello Marta, so glad we can finally get together and crunch these numbers." Lance announced as he made his way toward Marta with his hand outstretched. He was wearing Armani, his absolute favorite. Today, he took extra care to look fly because he was meeting with the sexy Marta VanDyke.

It wasn't just that she was sexy, she had that hands down, but she was smart as well as white. There was something about white women that turned Lance on.

He'd had his share of the sistahs but he tired of them quickly. He never found a fulfilling relationship with a black woman. Lance found them to be too demanding and controlling. For him, white women were just the opposite. With them, he was the one in control and making all the demands.

Touching Marta's hand, he found it to be soft and laughed slightly as he let her hand go.

"I'm sorry, did I miss some type of joke?" Marta asked with a hint of attitude.

Still chuckling, Lance thought to himself, *Feisty I see, well she can be tamed just like all the others.* "I was just thinking that after all of these years, this is the first time that you and I have had the opportunity to sit down and talk business." Lance hit Marta with his sexiest smile as he sat down at the table and began pulling files out of his leather satchel.

That's when it hit Marta, right when he flashed that choir boy, Colgate smile at her that Lance was hitting on her. This caused Marta to smile on the inside, not because she was interested, but because she thought she might have found her way in. Looking at Lance with her bedroom eyes glued to him, Marta crossed her legs, showing more of herself than she normally would and said, "Well let's get down to business, shall we."

Jason's Lyric
The last two days had been difficult for Jason. Charmaine was calling his phone non-stop and Bri wasn't answering any of his calls or texts; he finally got fed up and gave her an ultimatum. Scratching his head as he stood on his deep, oak deck overlooking his lush, green lawn, Jason was trying to understand where the conflict in his marriage was coming from. Until he met Bri, he had never met a woman before that he wanted to cherish and put before himself. Now shit was all mixed up and he really didn't know what he wanted to do.

Today, he spoke with Tony, his older brother, to try to get some perspective. It wasn't often that he shared his personal life with Tony, but he trusted his brother's opinion and discretion. Jason came clean, he told Tony about the *Open Marriage* that Bri proposed before they got engaged and about his willingness to indulge in it. He went on to tell Tony about wanting the arrangement to stop and how that revelation pushed Bri away. None of that was embarrassing for Jason to tell his brother, but when he told him about Charmaine, he felt the lowest of the low.

The Matthews men were brought up to revere their wives. To his surprise and delight, his brother didn't go in on him like he thought he would. Instead, he asked a simple but prolific question, *Do you love her?* It took the wisdom of his older brother to see past all the mistakes and the questionable decisions and ask the one question that really mattered. Taking a deep breath, the only answer Jason could provide to the question was yes. Tony told him it was as simple as that.

Then he went on to tell Jason how important it was to fight for his marriage. The sun was setting and Jason was finally feeling like he had some balance regarding his decision.

Luther Ingram blared from the home surround sound. Jason relaxed on the outdoor chaise and slowly bobbed his head to the lyrics.

If loving you is wrong, I don't wanna be right
If being right means being without you
I'd rather be wrong than right

Jason knew the basis of the song was about a married man in love with another woman. Although that exact analogy didn't fit his situation, the lyrics of the song touched him deeply because they focused on a love so deep that a man would risk everything. It was that type of love that he had for Bri. Closing his eyes, Jason allowed the music to flow though his body. Before he knew it, he had fallen asleep. He never felt his cell phone vibrate on his hip.

By the time she pulled into her driveway, it was well after 6 p.m. The long drive allowed her to do some soul searching on how to reconcile the demons from her past. When she walked into the home, Luther's "A House Is Not A Home" was blaring from the speakers. There was no voice like Luther's. Bri walked slowly through her home as if she hadn't seen it in ages. She was rubbing her hands on furniture as she walked and looking around as if everything was new.

Was it new or was the way she saw things becoming clearer in her mind, causing her to view things as if they were new? She had time to really think as she drove home.

Watching the sad existence that her mother lived scarred her deeply. Bri tried to save herself from that same pain.

In doing so, she may have damaged the most successful relationship she had ever had. Making her way to her bedroom, she hurriedly took a shower. She knew she was going to have to face Jason, but she wouldn't do it smelling like another man.

As the water steamed down her back, Bri decided if she wanted to salvage her marriage, she was going to have to come clean with Jason. She would have to tell him how much her childhood still affected her as an adult. The thought of voicing it out loud to someone else terrified Bri; she'd spent all of her adult life not being afraid of anything.

"At least you had enough respect to clean that nigga off you before you got in my bed." Seeing Bri in the shower made him sick to his stomach. Jason knew exactly what that meant.

The water shut off suddenly as Bri rolled her eyes with water dripping down her body.

She was feeling really emotional. Therefore, the last thing she wanted to do was argue with Jason.

What she really wanted was for him to simply hold her and together they would figure out how to repair what they both had a hand in breaking.

Stepping out of the shower, she expected to find him standing there giving her the evil eye, but he was nowhere to be seen. The music switched to Miles Davis; he was Jason's absolute favorite.

My funny valentine, sweet comic valentine
You make me smile with my heart
Your looks are laughable,
un-photographable
Yet, you're my favorite work of art

Bri sang the lyrics to herself as she listened to Miles blow his horn. The jazz version of the popular song was one that Jason played when he was going through something. The instrumental was kind of depressing yet, beautiful at the same time.

Walking into the bedroom, she could see Jason in the bed with a glass of brown liquor. To her surprise, there was a glass of white wine sitting on the nightstand waiting for her. Bri could see a longing in Jason's eyes, but she didn't quite know what to say, so he beat her to the punch.

"I'm not gonna front like I'm not pissed, 'cause I am. But I love you enough to find out if there is enough of us left to make this marriage work. So let's talk."

Silly Rabbit

Sitting outside of Jason's home might seem a bit extreme to some but to Charmaine, it was perfectly normal behavior. When Bri didn't return her text, she grabbed her purse and left the office to make sure her man was not consorting with the enemy. It bothered her that Jason was not answering his phone. She couldn't imagine why he wouldn't answer her call unless Bri had hidden his phone or shut it off completely. It was as if speaking her name caused her to appear. The GSF Lexus that Bri casually bragged that she had recently gotten pulled into the driveway. Charmaine slammed her open palm on the dashboard, pissed as she yelled, *I want this bitch out of my house today or I'm gonna burn the bitch down, simple as that!* Grabbing her phone, she shot a text message to Jason.

6:25 p.m. **My patience is wearing thin. I see this bitch pulling up in what should be MY car, into what should be MY driveway and walking into what should be MY goddamn house!**

I am giving you until tomorrow morning to get rid of her or I will! Think I'm playing, FUCK WIT ME!

With her hands shaking, Charmaine threw her cell phone on the passenger seat. Gripping the steering wheel tightly, she tried to calm herself. Her tires screeched as she sped out of the upscale neighborhood with tears forming in her eyes. If she was being honest with herself, she would say she was always on the fucked up end of a situation, but now was not the time for honesty.

In Charmaine's mind, now was the time to get what was hers in the first place. Jason was her man and Bri was just a silly rabbit who was about to find out that tricks were for kids. She felt it was up to her to free her man from the evil bitch that bewitched him.

Charmaine used her time at the traffic light to reflect on her image in the rearview mirror, thinking to herself, *I'm a bad bitch and I'ma get my man.* The woman she saw staring back at her held a lifetime of regret. It was a woman who had made some costly mistakes. But she also saw a woman whose time had come, so that's the woman she gravitated to. Pulling up to her condo, she felt refreshed.

There were no more tears to cry. Now there were only plans to be made. The day after tomorrow, she would accompany Bri to New York to present the new cosmetic line to the fashion week board. If Jason had not taken care of the problem by then, she would. Whatever happened, Charmaine planned to make sure that Bri was no longer a problem.

Last Duke Standing
Startisha and Jakari spent the entire evening studying the files from Duke's computer. The files were separated into two categories, company memos and work product. They both learned a lot about the inner workings of the company by reading through all of the files. Startisha smiled as she finished reading the last document.

"I'm glad to see you smiling Star, but we didn't find much to work with here." Jakari was scratching his head as he clicked in and out of different documents.

The smile didn't dim with his revelation, it actually got brighter. "I know Kari, its' just that looking through all of this stuff is somehow making me feel like I belong, like I'm privy to the family business. I don't know if that makes sense, but it feels kind of good." Startisha leaned over and gave him a really big kiss.

It felt really good to make his woman happy. However, Jakari wanted to do more than that, he wanted the Dukes to pay for the way they treated her. It hurt like hell for him not to be able to be there for her after her father died. Startisha was loss and he was locked up; he felt like shit.

The more she told him about how she was being treated, the more Jakari promised himself that one day they would pay. He was kind of pissed that they didn't find anything useful in the files. As he clicked out of the work product file, Jakari noticed an anomaly. The screen appeared to shake slightly. If your eyes weren't sharp, you would have missed it, but it was hard to get shit by Jakari. The only time he'd seen something like that occur was when there was an encrypted file.

Jakari began to run several locator programs to locate the file, but was having no luck. So he placed a call to the guru, the hack master, his boy, Lucky. Jakari learned all of his skills from his boy. However, he still had levels to go before he was a grand master like Lucky.

"Yo, if it isn't Mr. Straight and narrow!" Lucky yelled into the phone.

Jakari spent a lot of time with Lucky as a kid. Lucky was about ten years older than Jakari, but he saw something special in the miniature computer geek. He took Jakari under his wing and worked with him extensively when he wasn't sniffing up Startisha's ass. It hurt Lucky to his heart when Jakari got himself locked up.

They had only been in contact twice since he was released, but it was quickly evident that Jakari still had what it took to be a computer genius. Lucky drilled him on some specifics that he couldn't work on while on lockdown; as usual, Jakari caught on like a champ. Lucky was the one who put in the good word for Jakari to secure the interview at Beauty Mark. It didn't surprise him at all that Jakari got the job; he was an ace with the computer and had the personality that would win over the business executive.

"Hey O.G., what you up to? I need your help on something top secret." Jakari got straight to the point. He knew once he said top secret, Lucky would be ready to get down to business. He lived for this type of shit. Jakari explained the slight screen shake that he saw to Lucky and could almost hear him salivating through the phone.

Jakari hit the speaker on the phone as Lucky began to walk him through decrypting the random data of the True Crypt program. He explained that the one glitch in their system was the shaking of the screen. A normal computer user wouldn't notice it, but a hacker surely would.

It was widely known among hackers that companies left this unfortunate loophole.

Even with that, True Crypt was still the best program for securing a company's confidential information. After running several programs, an undetected file opened up. A big smile formed across Jakari's face as he yelled out, "Awww shit Lucky, we done opened up some shit! That's what I'm talking about! Hey man, thanks so much. Let me and Star go through all of this shit and I'll hit you back." Jakari watched Startisha approach him with a look of wonder in her eyes.

Lucky was curious about what Jakari was up too but decided to let it go until he was ready to share. "Ok youngster, hit me up if you need me."

After hanging up the phone, Jakari looked at a curious Startisha and said, "I think we hit the mother load, baby. Let them try and deny you now, you'll be the only Duke left standing."

There was a plumber's truck parked as discreetly as possible across the street from Startisha's home. The man inside was pointing a directional mic toward the house and taking notes as he listened intently. It was all the confirmation he needed that it was time to put his murder game down again.

Bri's Time

Bri was in the office early on the morning she was to leave for NY. There was so much that needed to get done before her flight was to leave. It felt good to finally feel some semblance of normalcy since her and Jason had a serious talk. They both were able to admit the harm they caused in their relationship by allowing other people to become part of their unit. Bri told Jason about her family, her father's attitude toward her and her mother as well as her mother's suicide. She tried to explain how those events helped shape her thought process and how she dealt with relationships and love. They talked through the night, it felt cleansing and refreshing. The love between them was still intact, but there was still work to do. They decided that Jason would come to New York later today, so they could have a second honeymoon. Spending lazy days in bed and burning the town up at night, would go a long way in healing their open wounds.

As she was finishing up in the office, she heard her text notification bell ring. Bri reached for the phone, wondering who was texting her at five in the morning.

5:10 a.m.   You thought I forgot about you bitch! I told you Jason is mine. He is my man, I am giving you one more opportunity to step the fuck off. Call him NOW and tell him you want a divorce or you will DIE!

Dropping the phone, Bri held her hands to her lips. She was shaking slightly but pulled herself together quickly. It did bother her that this chick was still trying to take her man, but to now threaten her life, shit had gotten very real.

135

Bri re-read the text again, making sure she wasn't hallucinating. Sure enough, it read the same. Jumping up from her seat, she grabbed her purse, checking inside to make sure her baby 9 was still in its place. One thing was sure, if this chick was texting her this early, she probably knew that Bri was the only one in the office. Thinking aloud Bri said, "I refuse to be a sitting duck for this bitch. If she shows her head, she gon' have a problem; I will put something special in her ass today."

Bri was about to call Jason but thought better. She knew he was still sleeping and also remembered his cell being on the kitchen counter when she left.

Shaking her head, she calmed herself some and decided to head to the airport and go through the lengthy check-in procedure. Even though she flew first class, after 9-11, everyone went through the same procedure, so she wasn't even mad at that. Her flight wasn't scheduled to leave until 8 a.m. Therefore, it would give her a chance to talk to Charmaine and make sure she had everything she was to bring with her to New York; her flight was leaving at 3 p.m. today.

Punching the ground button on the elevator, Bri made sure to look over her shoulder and observe her surroundings. It was quiet on the penthouse floor giving off an eerie vibe. The ding of the elevator caused Bri to jump slightly. Taking a deep breath, Bri fixed her burgundy Dolce pencil skirt; this helped to compose her as she moved forward into the elevator. Letting out a breath, she couldn't help but chuckle at herself.

Here she was the CEO of a major cosmetic company and married to a handsome and very successful owner of a fortune 500 advertising agency, and she was looking over her shoulder ready to shoot someone on sight. Bri decided to forget all about the foolishness and get her head back in the game.

When the elevator opened, she held her head high and started for her car, but she wasn't stupid, her left hand was in her purse.

Standing on the side of the pillar in the parking lot, was perfect for a good view of the elevator. The text sent to Bri was a surefire way to get her to leave the office quickly. The time had come; it was time to take a stand. It was time to let Bri know once and for all that she couldn't have Jason anymore. It was time to let the world know that Jason had always belonged to someone else. As Bri stepped out of the elevator and started moving toward her car, there was movement in her peripheral, but the swiftness of the movement took her by surprise. Bri was placed in a sleeper hold before she could even think about pulling out her gun. Her purse was quickly removed and dropped right next to her car then she was dragged to a non-descript van right next to her car. As best she could, she kicked and twisted but there was no escape. Bri was slammed against the van door so hard the wind was knocked out of her. It actually took some of the fight out of her. Duct tape was placed over her mouth and her hands were bound with zip ties.

It felt really good to finally be taking a stand against the one person that stood in the way of happiness. Bri's limp body was thrown in the back of the van. Jumping in the driver's seat and cranking the van up, the tires smoked, making a quick exit from the Glamour Girls' parking lot. Today would be a day of eternity for some but a day of death for others.

Who's Your Daddy?
Her body ached from her feet to her ears. It was a strange pain mixed with tingling sensations that were still causing her legs to shake. Marta stretched her arms over her head as far as they would go and yawned when she heard, "You ready for round five?" The thickness in Lance's voice caused her insides to immediately get wet.

Leaning into his strong, chiseled frame, Marta smiled and nestled her nose into his back. Her plan was to throw some good pussy on Lance and get him to partner with her to take over Glamour Girls and Beauty Mark. What she didn't expect was for Lance to put that dick on her so tough that she was spooning him like a newlywed.

"I asked you a question bitch." Lance said with just enough force to cause Marta to jump back as he turned to face her. Lance could see the anger trying to flare up in Marta because she was turning red. But before she could go into her sister girl act, he scooted down on the bed and jerked her legs apart aggressively. Staring at him was the pinkest pussy he had ever seen, it was beautiful and he planned to eat it every chance he got. Diving in head first, Lance ate Marta like it would be his last meal.

She was screaming from ecstasy as she pushed his shoulders trying to get him to stop his lustful attack, but Lance wouldn't stop; he planned on owning her body then her mind.

You see, Lance knew white girls like Marta; she was a closet freak who tried to act all buttoned up but really would take dick in like a prize fighter knocked niggas out.

Normally, Lance wouldn't give it or even let her smell it, but she was trying to play him. So for that, she had to get it Duke style. While her breathing was still labored and her legs still shaking, Lance climbed up her body pinning both of her legs near her ears. With one swift motion, he pushed 8½, thick inches of dick to the hilt. His plan was to clog up any will that she had to resist him. Lance dug deep, slamming his thighs against her pink round ass. "That's right bitch, take daddy's dick. Tell me you love this dick…tell me!" Lance demanded forcefully as he power-drilled into her.

When Marta didn't say anything right away, Lance pulled all the way out, sat back on his knees, and glared into her eyes.

He left her pussy pulsating and leaking at the same damn time. They were playing a game of eye spy until he heard exactly what he wanted.

"I love this dick; I love this dick!" Marta said, breathing heavily as she reached around trying to grab his dick.

Lance smiled to himself as he swatted at her hands. He knew he was right about her. Placing her right leg on his shoulder, Lance slammed his dick back into her without regard for her comfort. He wasn't there to make love to her. She wanted to be fucked and that's exactly what she was gonna get. He could hear Marta moaning loudly as she said, "Fuck me daddy! Yesssssss fuck me!"

And that's precisely what he did. At last count, Marta was on her fourth nut. The waterfall that was soaking his groin and legs was proof of that.

Lance could feel that sensation in the tip of his dick, so he went harder to reach his intended destination. As his nut was traveling up his shaft, he pulled out and moved quickly, grabbing Marta's head and forcing his dick into her mouth. To his surprise and delight, Marta sucked the nut right out of him, causing him to yell out,

"Suck this motherfucka bitch! Got damn...shit...shit...shit..." Lance fucked her face as all of his seeds were spilling from her mouth. It was the sexiest shit he had ever seen.

Breathing hard and watching Marta plant kisses all over his mushroom head of a dick, Lance said, "What's the plan bitch?"

A New York Minute

Manhattan is the most crowded of the five boroughs of New York City. It is also where most of the action happens. It's the epicenter of New York Fashion Week where buyers and the press can ogle over the latest international fashion collections. Park Avenue in Midtown Manhattan is home to the Waldorf Astoria, one of the most luxurious hotels in Manhattan. The hotel has 47 floors and was once the tallest hotel in the world. This is the setting for the fashion week board to decide which products would be used for the fashion week season. Bri also planned to use the platform to show the new face of Glamour Girls. Prior to this event, she sent out a press release to New York's popular fashion press. They were all present to see what the hype was about.

Charmaine was overseeing the setup in the grand atrium, and grand it was. There was a massive backdrop of the New York night skyline. There was a deep, dark red carpet commanding the attention of anyone in its view. On each side of the carpet, there were four, black, backless, swivel chairs.

There would be eight models showcasing the latest and greatest in the Glamour Girls' line.

The hottest makeup artists were on tap to work their magic. But the highlight of the evening would be the revealing of the new face of Glamour Girls. This would be the model that was chosen by Glamour Girls' fans to represent the brand for the year. Kishara, the current face of Glamour Girls was in town to hand over her crown.

This year would be a little different because there would also be the announcement about the merger with Beauty Mark, who would focus on the mainstream beauty products and Glamour Girls would continue to kill the black beauty market. After completing her supervision of the stage setting, Charmaine went to make sure that the dinner reception was on track. As she entered the atrium, she spotted Jason out of the corner of her eye. She smiled a little, but immediately got pissed when she thought to herself, *He never comes to these events, so if he's here, he's with her.* Charmaine's mood quickly went from sugar to shit as she stomped toward the ballroom.

Jason noticed Charmaine giving him the evil eye but tried to ignore it, he had more pressing and important issues like finding out where Bri was. He had been calling Bri for the last hour; he was starting to get worried.

Bri always answered his call unless she was pissed with him about something. The last time he checked, they were in the middle of working things out. Jason searched his brain, trying to think of where she could be when he saw Marta, Duke, and Lance huddled talking shop. He decided to see if any of them knew what was going on with Bri. Jason noticed how Marta looked at him as he approached; it was practically a look of disgust. He barely knew the chick, so he couldn't imagine what her issue was. As soon as he got close to them, all discussion stopped. It was kind of uncomfortable, but he was looking for his wife so he didn't care what their issue was.

"Hey everyone, sorry to interrupt you guys, but I'm looking for Bri. Has anyone seen or heard from her since you got to New York? Jason was looking at each of them, noticing the only one who looked indifferent was the dude he didn't know.

Duke was acting a little standoffish and Marta still had the same stank expression on her face.

Lance didn't know who the dude was but he could tell Duke didn't like him, and it was evident that Marta had a bug up her ass.

Instead of letting the dude stand there looking like an ass, Lance decided to break the stalemate and introduce himself. "Hello, I'm Lance Duke, nice to meet you." Lance greeted as he shook hands with Jason.

While the others looked at him like he had shit on his face, Jason shook hands with Lance. "Thank you Lance, I'm Jason, Bri's husband. She was supposed to fly in this morning, but she wasn't on the flight and hasn't checked into our hotel room. I'm starting to get worried about her." Jason watched Marta and Duke closely because they were acting weird as shit.

Duke's cell phone rang. After looking at his screen, he looked at Lance hard then walked away. Marta was watching the interaction between Duke and Lance with much curiosity. She watched as Lance's eyes followed Duke and made a mental note to get to the bottom of what was going on.

The irritating sound of Jason's voice brought her attention back. "So Marta, you haven't answered my question. I mean you are Bri's business partner, where is she?" Jason's voice sounded a little more demanding as he was nearing the end of his patience meter.

She didn't see a need to be cordial with Jason; she didn't like him and he might as well know it. With her hands on her hips and fire in her eyes, Marta turned all the way toward Jason and said, "Why are you even here? No one wants you here, not even Bri. If she did, she would be here. Go back to Virginia and let us run our business. If and when she wants to call you, she will with yo thirsty ass?" Marta turned to walk away before Jason could say anything. The smile on her face felt good, she had not smiled in months; she felt like she was finally in control.

The vibrating of his phone was the only thing that stopped Jason from slapping the shit out of Marta. He reached for his cell as she turned and twisted away. Flipping to his text message, he could see it was a video message. He opened the video to see Bri tied to a huge, four poster bed. She was stripped naked and appeared to be unconscious.

A tear immediately slid down his face, it pained him to see his beautiful, strong wife looking so helpless. The sound of a mysterious and distorted voice echoed through the video.

"For years, I have watched you worship someone other than me. It wasn't easy, but I did it because I love you. I even tried to move on with my own life and be happy for you, because I love you. But the pain of watching you love another is just too much, so although it may sound cliché, if I can't have you...no one can have you."

A pillow could be seen moving toward Bri's face. Jason cursed loudly, causing others to look his way. The mysterious voice started to speak again.

"If you want this bitch to live, you need to get here and tell her to her face that you're done with her and that you love only me. I'm only giving you three hours to do it. After that, she's one dead bitch. Where is here you ask? Meet us at the place where you had your best nut ever. If you come to the right place, I've proven my point." With that, the screen went black.

Jason fell to his knees right in the middle of the atrium, holding his head down breathing hard as his mind raced to find his next move.

Lance, who had watched the exchange between Marta and Jason with little interest, noticed Jason fall and was heading over to see if he was ok. However, he noticed Duke moving swiftly across the room with a determined look on his face. Lance abandoned his stride toward Jason when he saw the hard nod that Duke gave him. He quickly began moving toward his cousin to see what he needed. That's what Lance did; he was like the clean-up man in the Duke family.

By the look on his cousin's face, there was something big that needed cleaned. Duke and Lance huddled in the corner in a heated conversation. They were unconcerned with anything going on around them. Thoughts of the merger were gone; thoughts of Bri and Marta were gone. The only concern was Duke's business. Shaking his head as Duke talked, Lance was getting heated. There was no way they could let this shit slide. The Dukes, well at least the younger Dukes, were not really the straight-laced brood the world thought they were.

The younger Dukes didn't stand for bullshit; they nipped any disrespect in the bud swiftly. Duke put both hands on his cousin's shoulders then they both gave each other a hard nod and Lance turned to leave.

Marta watched the entire exchange between Duke and Lance. It pained her not to be able to hear what they were saying. As soon as Lance started heading quickly toward the exit, Marta tried to head him off. She wanted to know what was going on, and if he was still going to help her steal Glamour Girls from Bri. Her face was red as she caught up with him in her seven inch Manolos. "Wait a minute Lance, where are you going so fast?" Marta inquired slightly out of breath.

Stopping in his tracks with a hint of disgust on his face, he turned to face Marta, wondering should he get rid of her as well. "Don't question me bitch; you only answer questions. Whatever you do, don't get me mixed up with that nigga over there." He said, pointing toward Jason who was just now picking himself up from the floor. "Now get your ass back in the game and don't worry about what the fuck I'm doing."

With that, Lance turned quickly and headed out of the atrium, leaving Marta standing there picking her face up off the floor.

Fixing her clothes and looking around, Marta was trying to look as if nothing had just occurred when she heard his voice.

"I don't know what the fuck that dude Lance said to your evil ass, but whatever it was, good. You dumb, jealous ass, white, pasty bitch!" Jason didn't even wait for her to reply, he needed to get the next thing smoking back to Virginia.

Once again, Marta was left looking and feeling like a fool. However, now she was pissed and even more determined to take what she felt she had earned; she would take Glamour Girls.

Captivity
Bri woke up tied to a bed in a dark space, naked and sweating. Her mouth was extremely dry and she felt sick to her stomach. She tried to sit up and immediately fell back to the bed. Screaming out was harder than she expected; all she made was a faint sound. The pounding in her head was sure to cause permanent damage. She pulled her arms as hard as she could but they were bound tightly by rope.

"There's no escape." A voice echoed loudly through the room.

There were speakers somewhere in the room. She opened her eyes and tried to see through the darkness. Her head was threatening to explode from the pain, but she was determined to get herself together. "Who are you, what do you want with me?" She managed to ask although faintly.

It seemed like forever as she waited for someone to answer. Bri looked around the room, trying very hard to see something, anything that would tell her where she was. A loud crackling sound ricocheted off the walls.

As hard as it was to do so, Bri attempted to be alert and focused. She needed to be in order to try and figure out what was happening to her.

"You know what?" A loud distorted voice bellowed through the darkness. "I should have killed you years ago, maybe even that first night at The Brinks Lounge." It was hard not to hear the disgust in the voice of the captor.

Bri racked her brain thinking to herself, *If this bitch is talking about The Brinks Lounge, then she's been at this for at least two years. Who the fuck does that?* Once again, she tried to pull herself free from the ropes, even more determined to break loose. It was the next statement that knocked the wind out of her sail.

"Jason has belonged to me since college. When he first set eyes on you, I almost didn't let him pursue you, but he assured me it was nothing but a fuck thing. Imagine how I felt when he decided to marry your stank ass." Next, there was a sudden loud screech and pop that came through the speakers.

Bri was attempting to wrap her head around what was happening. Her mind was spinning, *what the fuck is going on; who the fuck is this; what the fuck is this?* She felt like crying but refused to show fear to whoever this freak was. Before she could reconcile her thoughts further, the door slammed open and a figure loomed. She couldn't see the person but she could smell, and the scent was faintly familiar.

"Jason is on his way. Once he gets here, you'll see that you were only temporary and your time has passed."

The distortion of the voice was gone; it was at that moment that Bri knew exactly who her captor was. *It couldn't be, could it? But why? What was this about?* She was confused and as all of the thoughts swirled through her mind, the voice kept getting closer.

"You should see your face–pitiful! You must really think he loves you girl. Poor little tink-tink. Jason can't love you when he loves me. He always has and he always will. It's not your fault though, my man is simply irresistible."

The smell of Issey Miyake crashed her nasal cavity and made it hard to deny what was becoming painfully obvious. The figure was now close enough for her to erase all doubt. Bri tried to sit up, refusing to play the victim any longer as she said, "Brent, how long have you and Jason been fucking." She watched as he moved all the way into her line of vision, taking a seat on the bed as if to reassure her of something.

Brent cleared his throat. He didn't feel like he owed her an explanation, but he needed her to understand that what she thought she had with Jason was over. "Jason and I have been together since college. We never called ourselves a couple or no gay shit like that, but we knew who we were to each other." He got up from the bed and moved around in the shadows of the room as he continued. "By the time Jason met you, he wanted to be "normal" do "normal" shit, but you fucked him up with your open marriage bullshit."

Bri let out a loud laugh, at least as loud as her sore throat would allow. It was a mixture between amusement and disgust. "So let me get this shit right.

You and Jason have been fucking since college, but he wanted some regular shit? Where did that leave you and urrrrgh what about Sonya and those babies!?

Fucking niggas make me sick to my stomach, I swear!"
Bri found herself ready to explode with furry. This is
exactly why she refused to give herself totally to anyone,
they were always on bullshit. She saw it growing up and
thought she learned the lesson from watching it destroy
her mother.

Brent was unbothered by Bri's outburst. He didn't expect
her to understand the relationship between him and
Jason. Once Jason got married, he basically begged Brent
to get married as well. He made it seem like it was
something they had to do. Brent didn't really want to
marry anyone other than Jason. When he met Sonya, she
was nice enough and not a bad looking woman, so he
went for it. Never in a million years did he expect to have
kids with her, but he loved his babies with everything.
Before he snatched Bri, Brent told Sonya he wanted a
divorce and told her why. Naturally, she went the fuck
off, but it is what it is. Brent vowed to still be there daily
for his kids, but he had to find his happiness as well.
"Don't worry about Sonya and my kids, they're good.
You just get ready to pack ya shit and get outta my man's
house. No hard feelings, but you can't really have what
belongs to someone else, can you?"

Before Bri could register her disgust further, the door
flew open in the darkness and crashed against the wall.
"This is not the way to handle this Brent?" Jason was
furious as he approached the bed.

He was giving Brent the evil eye while he worked on the
knot on Bri's right hand, cursing under his breath. The
look in Bri's eyes were not missed by Jason; he knew she
was pissed off.

He could only imagine what Brent had already told her. For that reason, he had to make sure she understood from his perspective. As he continued to work on releasing her, he tried to explain. "Bri, I know this may seem fucked up to you, but I need you to know that I love you baby. I just happen to love Brent too." He watched Bri's eyes pop open even wider than they already were as he continued. "When I was asking you to stop having an open marriage and just concentrate on each other, I had already made the decision to commit to only you. I was letting Brent go, but I needed that same commitment from you baby, can't you see?"

Jason ignored the gasp coming from Brent's direction as he ran from the room. He made the decision that he wanted a life like his parents and siblings. He didn't want to be with a man or have a wife that needed sex with other people. He wanted one woman, a loving relationship, and children. As he untied the last rope, he was pleading with his eyes, hoping that Bri would give him a chance. Regrettably, all he saw was her head moving from one side to the other.

It was hard for Bri to listen to what Jason was telling her without being disgusted. She was pissed that he even invited her into his world, knowing his heart belonged to someone else. Bri was a very liberal woman, but there was no way she would even attempt to compete with another man. *Fuck love; love is for suckas*, Bri thought to herself as she shook her head back and forth. Bri had to admit that she was pissed with herself for even letting herself get in this predicament. Nonetheless, she was about to correct it. Finally free from her ropes, she moved slowly to sit up.

The pain in her movements were evident, but she refused to give into it. She swatted at Jason's hands as he tried to help her. Her voice, although unstable, was clear enough to get her point across.

"Don't you fucking touch me, fuck is wrong with you!" Bri braced her arms on the bed as she lifted herself to the floor. Her eyes darted through the darkness, attempting to find her clothes as she continued. "I'm done and I don't wanna hear another fucking word from you or your...man!"

Bri noticed her clothes thrown across a chair in the corner and began moving in that direction with as much grace as she could under the circumstances. Jason jumped up from the bed and raced ahead of her, grabbing the clothes before she could reach them. He knew if he held the clothes he could at least get her to hear him out, and right now, he really needed her to listen to him. They were just getting back on track and he didn't want something as trivial as this to sidetrack them. Holding her clothes out of reach he said, "You can't mean that Bri. We have shared so much together, we can get through this. I want us to get through this, baby; I swear I love you so much."

Jason was bordering on begging. However, with the way he was feeling, he wasn't too proud to beg at this point. He wanted to get things on track with Bri.

The loud clapping caught both Jason and Bri by surprise. They both turned their attention toward the interruption.

Jason immediately jumped in front of Bri to shield her from the horror they now faced.

"My heart is shattered to see you run to this bitch and beg her to stay with you. You have always been all the man I needed, but you've made it painfully obvious that I'm no longer all that you need." Brent was pointing a gun and sounding deranged. He had a crazed look in his eyes, and it looked like he was crying. Jason blamed a lot of this on himself; he knew how much Brent loved him, and for the record, he loved him also. But Jason needed more and he could never get Brent to understand that. When Brent got married, Jason hoped like hell he was finally willing to bury anything other than a friendship between them. After his children were born, Jason was certain that Brent had moved on. Looking at the extreme circumstances that he was going through now killed any hope of that. Jason held his hand up toward Brent as he started to talk.

"I'm sorry Brent. This is all my fault. Bri has nothing to do with this, so just let her go and you and I will talk about what to do about us."

The tension in the room was thick. Bri was trying her best not to pop off, but she wasn't stupid, she could see the gun and crazed look in Brent's eyes. Out of the corner of her eye, she was trying to locate her purse but didn't see it anywhere. Bri was hoping Jason could talk him down or she was going to have to improvise.

The unmistakable sound shook the room. Bri saw the smoke rising from Jason's shoulder before either of them realized he was shot. Still trying to shield Bri from harm, Jason dropped to one knee. He was bleeding profusely from his shoulder but refused to fold. "Brent stop this now, this is not you. We're better than this, now stop." Jason was breathing hard as he tried to talk sense into Brent.

Whatever Jason was trying to do wasn't working. Bri felt like they were sitting ducks and she was ready to do something different. She was perched behind Jason as he tried to shield her even though he was in a lot of pain.

For a second, Bri felt sorry, but then she remembered how they got in this position in the first place.

As she knelt behind Jason, she could hear him still pleading with Brent and was disgusted. There was something in the small of Jason's back that caught her attention.

Bri cursed under her breath when she realized it was a gun. Without further discussion, Bri pulled the gun from Jason's back and started to fire. The room was chaotic as bullets were flying everywhere. The only other sound was Jason screaming, "Nooooooooooooooooooo!"

Betrayal
Hours after the discovery of the files, Jakari and Startisha were still in a state of shock. They had spent most of the evening kicking around ideas of how to handle the situation. Startisha's emotions had been all over the place. She still didn't want to believe that her brother could be so hateful, but it was hard to deny. Throwing the now printed files down, she jumped up from the couch and started pacing back and forth. Jakari merely watched; he wanted to let her vent.

"Kari, this just don't make no sense. Duke and Poppa were beefing to the point where Poppa was gonna cut Duke off. I mean damn, Duke is playing it like he was this perfect son when he's really the devil in disguise. Urrrrrgh, I'm so pissed Kari, I swear." Plopping back down on the couch, she put her head in her hands and started to cry.

It hurt him to his heart to watch the love of his life cry. It seemed like all the Dukes did was make her cry.

Jakari spent most of his time, along with her mother, trying to reassure Startisha that she was good enough to be a Duke. Right now, he didn't feel like the Dukes were good enough for her.

From what he knew about the bunch, they were racist and adulterers, and judging from the memo sent to Duke from Poppa Duke, they were heavy gamblers. Poppa Duke confronted Duke about him putting the family business in jeopardy with his gambling.

157

It turns out that Duke owed money from Atlantic City all the way to Vegas, and people were going to Poppa Duke to collect. It got even worse; Duke answered his father's memo by sending one of his own. In it, he cursed his father for having another family. He called his father a liar, a cheater, and a disgrace to the Duke name. The kicker was the threat; that's what had both Jakari and Startisha fucked up. In the memo, Duke said it wouldn't be hard for a sixty-five year old man to die from what would appear to be natural causes. Duke closed out the letter by saying he didn't want any more problems or that would be the last problem he had. Shaking his head as he cradled a crying Startisha, Jakari was ready to put Duke's ass on blast.

"He killed my Poppa, Jakari." Startisha sobbed as she spit the words out and cried into Jakari's shoulder.

It was the only conclusion they could make after reading the file. Not only did they read the damaging memo, but there was account information that showed thousands of dollars being transferred out of business accounts and into Duke's personal accounts the day after Poppa Duke died. More files showed payments being made to different people in Vegas, Atlantic City, Dover, Baltimore, West Virginia, and Reno. Jakari had Lucky look into the names of the people the payments were made to, all of which were bookies. Not just any kind of bookies, they all were associated with the Lupo Syndicate, who were all leg breakers and killers. Jakari kissed her forehead as she continued to release her anger and pain onto his shoulder.

"It's going to be alright baby. We're gonna make him pay for this Star, believe that."

"I'm sorry to hear that; I really am." Both Jakari and Startisha jumped at the raspy voice of an intruder.

The loud scream from Startisha vibrated off the living room walls. It was ear-piercing and filled with terror. So caught up in their own shit, they never even heard them enter. Sure enough, standing in the left corner was a man holding a gun, wearing a ski mask. Standing in the right corner was another man also holding a gun, but without a mask. Jakari knew when a man showed his face he didn't plan on leaving any witnesses.

"Fuck y'all doing in my house, dude?" Jakari said with venom seeping from his tongue as he swiftly moved a shaking Startisha behind him on the couch.

Lance chuckled at the lil nigga who was protecting his lil cousin. He didn't know Startisha personally, but he knew who she was. He knew that his uncle was smashing Glenda. Hell, he's the one who broke the news to Duke. That's what he did; Lance was in charge of keeping tabs on all the Dukes. He knew about his cousin Duke's gambling, his Uncle Duke's mistress and bastard, his father's drinking, and his sister's lesbian affairs.

He was keeper of the family secrets as well as the muscle who took out anyone who dared to challenge the Duke family; even a Duke.

"This is cute but no one cares. You two are not a factor, but you've stumbled onto sensitive family information, so that makes you dangerous–no correction that makes you dead."

That last statement stirred something in Startisha. Before Jakari could stop her, she pushed him off of her and jumped up, yelling with fire in her eyes. "I am part of this family you stupid motherfucker. I am a Duke; and who the fuck are you to come into my home and tell me any different. GET THE FUCK OUT!"

Lance had to admit, he liked her spunk; but in the grand scheme of things, she didn't matter. With the information she had, she could ruin everything they'd been working for over the last couple of years. Lance was not here to debate; he was a solution-focused guy whose solutions were permanent. "Who am I? I'm your cousin, Lance Duke. Nice to meet you Startisha Duke." He uttered his last declaration just as shots rang out through the house.

The Show Must Go On

It was time for the big event, Charmaine's last minute preparations were evident in the extraordinary outcome. The face models were in place, the makeup artists were on point, and the Fashion Week board was on deck. The atrium looked beautiful, just like New York City night life; it was perfect and the reporters and fashion week fans were in the house. The DJ was playing the latest chart toppers as Marta and Duke took to the stage with microphones in their hands. The music began to fade out and Marta started her announcements. "Welcome everyone to the Glamour Girls' showcase. We put this showcase on every year for the Fashion Week board so that they can decide on which products they may want to possibly feature during the fashion week season. This year, we are going to do things a little different. We have some special announcements that we will make today. Of course, there will be a changing of the guard of last year's face of Glamour Girls. Kishara, will be handing over the crown to this year's winner. But Duke, of Beauty Mark, Inc., also has another big announcement to make.

So sit back and enjoy yourself as we get things popping." Marta and Duke waved to the crowd as they stepped off the stage.

Charmaine watched from the sideline as Marta was helped off the stage by Duke. She hated both of their guts; all of them made her ass itch. Her anger was at its peak since Jason nor Bri were present. It didn't take much for her imagination to picture where they were.

161

Charmaine promised on everything that today was the last day she would be the other woman; she was confronting Bri tonight. She watched as each model paraded her Glamour Girls face in front of the panel. The crowd was going wild, watching the bombshells walk the runway. They paused in front of the board and gave them face. The approval was written all over the face's of the board members as they watched glamour look after look. It was apparent that this year's line was a hit; the makeup artists had performed their magic as well. The last model to walk was Kishara, last year's Face of Glamour Girls. When she walked, the crowd stood to their feet. Over the year, her face had been everywhere, from billboards to commercials. Everyone knew who Kishara was now.

When Kishara stopped in front of the board, she was handed a microphone then the music faded as she began to speak.

"Hello everyone! Wow, what a marvelous time we are having tonight! From the bottom of my heart, I want to thank Glamour Girls for giving me the opportunity last year to grow with a wonderful organization. I am so excited about passing the torch to a wonderful young lady who will represent Glamour Girls with so much grace. You guys are going to love her. Help me give a big Glamour Girls welcome to Lucretia." Kishara stepped aside, clapping her hands as Lucretia started her mean walk down the runway.

Lucretia was especially fly in her royal blue Givenchy lace pants suit. She walked like she owned the stage and the crowd was eating it up.

Marta and Duke watched with approval as they prepared to shock the crowd with their merger announcement. Marta decided it was now or never to make her move. She didn't know where Lance was or even if he was going to back her play. Nevertheless, for her, it was tonight or never.

Lucretia was blowing kisses to the crowd as she waved and exited the runway. The music was festive and the crowd hype as Marta and Duke took the stage again.

They both agreed that Duke would start the announcement off. He was looking dapper as usual, but something was distracting him. Although she hated his guts, she wanted to know what was going on with him.

"We definitely want to thank everyone for coming out tonight, and we have one more announcement to make." Not knowing what was about to be said, the crowd screamed as Duke continued. "It is with great pleasure that Glamour Girls, Inc. and Beauty Mark, Inc. would like to announce the merger of our two companies. With both powerhouses working together, we will continue to bring you more of the best in beauty products." The crowd was going wild as Duke bowed to Marta to speak.

As Marta waved to the crowd, they began to quiet down a bit to let her speak. She was a little nervous as she stared out at the crowd. This was a big step for her, but she finally felt in control. Bri, Jason, Duke, and even Lance would have to learn to bow down to the new queen.

"Wow, what a night ladies and gentlemen! On behalf of Glamour Girls and Beauty Mark, now known as Glamour Beauty Girls, Inc., we want to thank everyone for coming out. Fashion Week board members, we hope we have given you something to think about for the upcoming Fashion Week season. There is just one more announcement to be made then we want you all to join us for food, drinks, and music." Marta took a deep breath before she continued; she needed to make this count. "Briann Jennings has decided to step down as CEO of Glamour Girls, Inc." There was a collective gasp and flashing bulbs coming from the crowd. Duke turned to Marta with a quizzical look, but tried to maintain a level of professionalism with a slight smile. The torch has been passed to me to carry on the tradition of excellence at Glamour Girls. We wish Bri and her husband, Jason, luck as they move into a new phase of their lives. Again, everyone thank you for coming and let's party!!!" Marta waved to the crowd and started to move toward the edge of the stage.

Charmaine had tears falling from her eyes; she knew she'd heard Marta right when she said Bri and Jason were moving in a new direction.

Bri was leaving the company to be with her man basically. Charmaine was hurt as she thought to herself, *That's why that BITCH isn't here! I swear, she'll go to any length to keep my man from me, and these bitches up in here are all in on it! They have all laughed at CHARMAINE for the last fucking time!*

Before the party could even get started, a loud boom could be heard over the music then the screams started. The music screeched to a halt and bodies started falling from the hail of gunfire. It was pure chaos. The only person who seemed to be in control was Charmaine as she sprayed the room with her automatic rifle while thinking, *Who's laughing now Bitches!*

Survival - A Week Later
You couldn't turn on the local or national news without hearing about the tragedies linked to Glamour Girls and Beauty Mark, Inc. Both companies had such a rich history and squeaky clean images. Hence, you could believe the media was having a field day. It was the arrest of Charmaine in the New York massacre that set the whole investigation spinning. She killed over thirty people, including Marta before she was tackled and held down, kicking and screaming until New York's finest could subdue her.

It took two days of interrogation before Charmaine began to weave a tale of sex, lies, and murder so wild that the New York authorities immediately contacted their Virginia counterparts to locate Briann and Jason Matthews to make sure they were safe. They still hadn't been able to talk with Duke as he was in a comma in a New York hospital.

Detective Raymond Colston was one of the rising stars in the Norfolk Police Department. He was on every Virginia Police Department's wish list; several had tried to entice him to transfer.

He didn't understand what all the fuss was about; he enjoyed his work and tried to do his best to keep the community safe–no big deal. But that's how Colston was; he underestimated his potential on the force, just like he did with women. It wasn't that he didn't think he was a good cop, because he did. It wasn't even that he thought he wasn't a handsome dude because he thought he looked alright. But he didn't understand why women were always acting all goofy when he entered a room.

You would think they had never seen a decent looking brotha before. Furthermore, he didn't understand why all of the special op's departments wanted him when there were plenty of officers with just as much skill as him. Thoughts like these often made him laugh to himself.

Colston recently caught a double homicide that was all over the media. He wanted to treat this one with kid gloves and close it quickly. If there was one thing he didn't like, it was the media. Colston was rushing to the King's Daughter hospital after receiving a call from the doctor letting him know that his patient was finally awake. There was a lot of freaky shit going on and he needed to get to the bottom of it.

Earlier today, he got a call from New York detectives requesting that Briann and Jason Matthews be located. The detectives explained that the Matthews were material witnesses in the New York Massacre. Colston had briefly seen news coverage about the shootings in New York, but he didn't put them together with his murders in Virginia.

Two days earlier, a traumatized Jason Matthews called 911 reporting a shooting. He was screaming at the operator and clearly distraught. When paramedics and police made it to his location, a shot rang out. Once the police cleared the scene, there were three bodies sprawled out on the floor, only one was still breathing.

Colston told the NY Detectives he would get back with them after he had more answers for them. Colston was waiting patiently in the emergency room for the doctor to grant him access; he really needed to get a grasp on what was going on.

As usual, the media was blowing stuff out of proportion especially with the shootings in New York. He wasn't convinced that one had anything to do with the other at this point. The vibration on his hip caused an inward sigh because it was never good news.

It had been two days since Glenda had heard from her daughter or Jakari. It was strange because they never went a day without contacting her. Glenda lived a quiet life away from the spotlight and that's how she liked it, but she kept in touch with her daughter and she loved Jakari like her own child. You would have to be a hermit not to know what was going on in the news. Consequently, Startisha and Jakari not calling her wasn't helping her nerves. She tried calling them numerous times but after both of their voicemails were full, Glenda made the decision to drive over to her daughter's house. What she found when she entered almost gave her a heart attack. Blood was everywhere; Glenda stifled a scream as she ran over to the bodies of her loved ones. Snatching her cell phone from her purse, she dialed 911.

There was no greater pain than to see death in your child's eyes. First her Duke, and now their baby. Shaking her head, Glenda felt as though it was too much for her to bear. She didn't know how she would make it through something like this. The knock on the door caused her to jump a foot high, but once she heard someone yell, "Police," she calmed down and ran to the door.

The paramedics rushed forward while the police attempted to calm a crying Glenda. The game changer came when one of the paramedics yelled out, "We got a pulse here!"

Detective Colston grabbed his phone from his waist. "Yeah, what ya got for me?" That was the way he always answered his phone. After listening intently, his attention was distracted by the commotion at the emergency room door. Doctors were running toward it as paramedics burst in pushing a gurney while yelling out information. The voice on the phone was telling him that the victim should be coming through the emergency room door any minute. Shaking his head, he hung up the phone and rushed toward the moving crowd yelling, "I'm Detective Colston, what do we have doctor?"

The doctor who was moving fast next to the gurney yelled out as he eyed the detective's credentials. "We have one Startisha Duke who presents with multiple gunshot wounds and a faint pulse."

Colston grabbed the doctor's shoulder, stopping him in his tracks and said, "Did you say Startisha Duke?" Colston's eyes were burning a hole through the doctor's skull.

The doctor actually looked scared as he nodded his head in the affirmative, confirming Detective Colston's question before rushing off to assist with the patient.

Pacing back and forth in the middle of the emergency room floor, Colston was scratching his head trying to wrap his head around what it meant for so much tragedy to simultaneously strike the Glamour Girls and Beauty Mark, Inc. families. He knew there was something that connected all of it, but, for the life of him, he couldn't make it out, saying out loud, "This is some strange shit."

He jumped slightly as he heard a voice behind him say, "Yes, it is strange detective. I've been watching the news and on everything I love, the Dukes have something to do with what happened to my baby." Glenda was trying to be strong for her daughter. Now she was ready to help get to the bottom of it. She approached the detective because she knew she could help.

With a perplexed expression on his face, Colston knew he heard her say, *my baby.* "I'm sorry ma'am, what's your name?

Are you Startisha's mother?" Colston was rambling but he really needed to get to the bottom of what was happening here.

Glenda nodded her head as she explained to the detective who she was and how her daughter became a Duke. She explained to Colston about the resentment of the family toward her daughter as well as her daughter's mission to make the Dukes recognize her as one of their own. The most interesting thing Glenda told Colston, was that her daughter had a hidden security system in her home; it was the one thing Glenda insisted on when her daughter first moved out.

Colston couldn't contain his excitement about the information Glenda had just given him. He immediately called the information in as he saw a doctor walking toward him. Then he turned and thanked Glenda for her assistance, promising to get back to her as soon as he had some answers. Colston moved swiftly to meet the doctor with an extended hand. "Hello doctor, I'm Detective Colston. Can I speak with the patient now?"

Colston realized he sounded impatient, but he had to put shit together and no time to waste.

The doctor whose name was Wallington told Colston he could see the patient for a short period and ushered him in the direction of the room. Thanking the doctor, Colston entered the room with #24 on the wooden door. The room smelled stale with a mixture of some type of antiseptic and perspiration. Colston walked near the bed where the patient appeared to be sleeping soundly, looking no worse for the wear. He stood there for a minute watching the breathing pattern, the rise and fall of the chest. Colston didn't make a sound and almost laughed out loud when the patient opened one eye to see who was in the room. "You wanna stop faking sleep now, Brent?"

****

Hours later in a New York hospital, Lance paced back and forth at his cousin's hospital bedside. He couldn't understand how shit went sideways in NY while he was in VA cleaning up a mess.

Some part of him felt guilty for not being there to help his cousin. Marta being dead was not even on his radar as he thought to himself, *I was gonna kill her ass anyway.*

The police informed him that the shooter, Charmaine, had already been arraigned and was denied bail. Lance learned that she was Bri's secretary. Outside of that, he didn't know much about her. The door to the hospital room opened and Jon Jon sashayed in.

"Heyyy Lance, how are you hun." Jon Jon knew he made Lance uncomfortable. It tickled him so much that he couldn't help but continue messing with him, so he waved.

All Lance could do was shake his head at Duke's persistence. Although he didn't like the fruity dude, he was aware that he had Duke's back. "What's up Jon Jon; and gon' with all your bullshit man. How do they say Duke is doing?"

Rubbing a cool cloth over Duke's head Jon Jon smiled slightly. "He's sleeping soundly now, just glad he's no longer in a comma; that shit had my nerves bad."

Jon Jon looked like he was about to cry as he continued, "I don't know what was wrong with that crazy bitch, but I want her ass dead." He removed the cloth and began fussing with the covers.

Lance had to smile a little bit. He would have never thought that his mind and Jon Jon's mind would be aligned for any reason, due to the fact that he wanted to wrap his hands around Charmaine's throat.

His phone vibrated in his pocket. "Yo, what's up?" He said into the phone, listening intently. Lance hung up the phone and looked down at his cousin with concern. Jon Jon was still fussing over him, Lance took comfort in that. "Jon Jon I gotta roll, something's come up. Take care of him and I'll be in touch."

Lance turned to leave before Jon Jon could ask any questions. He knew it would only be a matter of time before they came for him.

What was done, was done, there was nothing he could do about it. Now he had to focus on survival; he had to disappear.

****

What a difference a day makes. Detective Colston spent the entire night at the hospital talking to Brent, who surprisingly was eager to provide information. He told Colston about him and Jason's love affair and how shattered he was when Jason married Bri.

Colston tried not to interrupt; he just turned on his recorder and let him talk.

"I tried to warn Bri to stay away from Jason but she wouldn't take heed so she had to go. I gave my life up for Jason. Then he chose her over me again and for that, his ass had to go. Since they wanted to be together so bad, they can be together in hell." Brent sat up in the hospital bed as far as he could as he made his point.

Colston told Brent what went down in New York and Brent let out a slight chuckle. He went on to enlighten him about Charmaine's infatuation with Jason and her hate for Bri.

The fact that Jason fucked her and was supposed to leave Bri for her may have been in Charmaine's head. At least it shed some light on why she went off the deep end. Standing and stretching a little, Colston was partially satisfied. Now he needed to understand what happened to Startisha.

One of the nurses had already informed him that she was out of surgery and doing better, so she was his next stop.

Taking his cuffs out, Colston cuffed Brent's wrist to the rail on the bed then read him his rights.

Brent had already prepared himself to the fact that life as he knew it was over. He knew there was no way he could fight his fate. He felt some vindication in the fact that the world would know that Jason once loved him. Brent watched the detective turn to leave just as the door to the room opened.

"Excuse me ma'am, this room is off-limits. Who are you?" Colston asked the beautiful woman who appeared in the doorway.

"She's my wife, Sonya." Brent said sounding frightened.

Sonya moved forward and shook Colston's hand as she said, "Detective, I won't be long. I just need Brent to sign these divorce papers.

Colston watched as Sonya pulled the papers and a pen from her purse and walked over to Brent like she didn't have a care in the world.

He had to admire her strength because he knew she was about to be a single mother to triplets. He made a note to himself to check in on her after the dust settled. Watching her closely, he could tell this was difficult for her.

Brent signed the papers and started to say something but Sonya held her hand up to stop him, folded the paper, placed it back in her purse, and turned to leave. "Thank you, Detective," was all Sonya said as she exited the room.

Detective Colston left the room without another word right behind her; he needed to talk to Startisha. The video from her house was viewed but he needed some answers that only she could provide. Taking the elevator up to room 450, Colston knocked on the door lightly before entering. He wasn't surprised to see her mother by her side comforting her. Startisha was crying as he entered. "Excuse me, so sorry to have to interrupt Ms. Duke. I am…"

Before he could get it out, Startisha said, "I know who you are. My mother told me you were here." She attempted to wipe her eyes and make sure she was covered completely at the same time. Her mother tried to help her.

Colston walked slowly toward the bed as he said, "Ms. Duke, I am so sorry to have to speak with you right now, but I have to get a better understanding of what happened to you and Jakari. I am so sorry for your loss. I want to catch these men who hurt you and killed Jakari. Can you help me?" Colston watched as tears fell from her eyes.

Startisha went on to tell the detective about Jakari stealing the files from Duke's computer as well as all of the information contained in the files. The tears started flowing heavily after she told him that Duke killed her father then sent her cousin Lance and another guy to kill her. Detective Colston couldn't believe what he was hearing. One of the guys in the video was Lance Duke and she was accusing Hudson Duke of killing his father. The case had just got wilder with every revelation.

Startisha could tell that he didn't believe her. Hell, she knew it was a lot to digest. Yet, here she was in the hospital and the love of her life, Jakari, was dead. Wincing in pain, she told the detective to check the files for himself. "If you go into Jakari's computer, you'll have access to all of the files I'm talking about." Startisha started to feel the medication she was given kick in as she closed her eyes.

Colston didn't get a chance to tell her that the computer was missing from the house. But he did plan on calling in a warrant for Beauty Mark and Glamour Girls. In the meantime, he put an APB out for Lance Duke, making sure to enter it in the NCIC database so that it would be picked up in every state. After saying goodbye to Glenda and promising to touch base with her, Colston left the room quickly with his phone glued to his ear. It was time to blow this investigation out of the water.

A Year Later - The Last Duke Standing
Glamour Girls, Inc., a year later, looked a lot different. It had been a long and trying year. When Duke was released from the hospital, he found himself under arrest for the murder of his father and conspiracy in the murder of Jakari and attempted murder of his sister, Startisha. The public embraced Startisha, they fell in love with her even more as all of the information came out at Duke's trial. Duke was convicted and was serving a life sentence. People Magazine had her on the cover with the caption *Last Duke Standing.* Tapping her pen on her desk, Startisha's mind thought back to the day she visited Duke in the holding cell right after the trial.

"Hello Duke," she stated as she walked close enough to the cell to touch the bars. She wasn't scared and needed him to know that. It was difficult for her to understand the level of hate that her brother had for her to go as far as he did.

"Well if it isn't the People's choice. Fuck you want Startisha, you won." Duke spit the venom from his mouth as he eyed the man standing guard.

She noticed him looking at the guard and figured if she wanted straight answers, she would need to get rid of him. Looking at the guard, she asked him if he could allow them to speak alone. The guard looked from Startisha to Duke before deciding he would wait right outside the door. Startisha assured him that if she needed him, she would yell for him. After the guard left, she turned back to Duke.

"Now you can stop with the bullshit and tell me why the fuck you tried to kill me dear brother." There was a hint of sarcasm in her voice, but definitely a sharp bite to her tongue.

Duke moved swiftly to the bar and grabbed her wrist before she could snatch it back. The fire in his eyes burned through her skull as he said, "Don't for a minute think I can't get to you from in here little sistah. I suggest you enjoy   your time in the Duke spotlight while you can because the game is almost over."

She pulled and pulled until she was able to snatch her wrist free of his grasp. His sinister laugh could be heard loudly as she ran from the holding room. Startisha was sure she could hear him all the way down the hall.

Duke was getting even more heated as he delivered his confident, cryptic laugh. However, deep inside, his world was falling apart. The only thing he needed right now was to reach out to the one man who could make some things happen for him; he needed to talk to Lance.

Thinking about that meeting with Duke made her skin crawl. She couldn't believe that her own flesh and blood would be so hateful towards her; but he was. There was nothing she could do about that, it took her some time to finally understand. In fact, Bri played a role in Startisha's recovery, because Startisha was surely a mess. With Jakari dead, she just felt damaged. A lone tear escaped her eyes and slid down her face as she slumped down in her chair and thought back to the day she learned to breathe again.

Open Marriage: A Fatal Attraction Story

The days leading up to the funeral of Jason and Briann Matthews was a media frenzy. Details of the tragedy was all anyone was talking about, especially Brent. He was giving exclusive interview from lock up, which in itself was unprecedented. He had one of the best attorneys in the state and with that came privileges.

And Brent didn't spare any details, nothing was off limits; including his relationship with Jason. The media ate it up and the public couldn't get enough.

Startisha was disgusted that Brent would run Jason and Bri's good names through the mud; it pissed her off. Initially she wasn't going to attend the funeral today, but as the sole heir to the Glamour Girl throne she really needed to pay her respects. The streets outside of Mt. Zion were crowded with spectators. Startisha didn't know if they were there because they genuinely mourned the loss of Jason and Bri or if they were just being nosey. Walking into Mt. Zion was overwhelming, it was standing room only. Startisha removed her shades and scanned the entire congregation for somewhere to sit. A tap on her shoulder caused her to jump lightly. Turning her head slowly, she let out the intake of breathe she was holding and smiled at Detective Colston.

> *"Hello Detective." She whispered.*

He offered a warm smile

> *"Hello Ms. Duke, it's good to see you. There is a section up front for the family, come with me. "*

Startisha didn't understand what Detective Colston was talking about, she wasn't family but she followed him anyway because he already started walking.

As she navigated the isle behind him she noticed how people where gawking and pointing in her direction. She felt a little uncomfortable and out of place, but held her head up high; she was a Duke. When they made it to a pew that was half empty, Detective Colston held his hand out like an usher.

"Here you go Ms. Duke."

He was turning to leave when he felt the tap on his shoulder. Turning he saw the uncertain look in Startisha's eyes as she said

> *"I'm sorry Detective Colston, I was just wondering if you would like to sit here with me?"*

To the lay person Startisha looked regal and like she had it all together, but Colston was an experienced detective, he could feel the nervous energy oozing from her pores. In an attempt to reassure her he smiled

> *"I can't right now Ms. Duke, I'm on duty. The Matthew's family wanted to make sure that no one interrupted their son's funeral.*
>
> *But everyone in this pew is a part of either Glamour Girl or Beauty Mark so you are in good hands." With that he smiled again and turned to leave.*

The sound of the organ coming to life caused her to snap to attention and immediately take her seat, picking up the obituary as she sat. Focusing on the immaculate looking choir wearing purple robes with gold tassels Startisha began to really take in her surroundings; the sounds, the smells, the regalia.

The choir began to sing a hymn that she could not place as she stared at the obituary. Staring back at her was Briann and Jason, it was a picture from their wedding. The looked happy and most importantly in love. Startisha found herself smiling at the couple as she read.

In Loving Memory of Briann Jennings-Matthews and Jason Matthews.

The obituary went on to describe the couples' lives separately and together. It wasn't missed on Startisha that Bri didn't seem to have a lot of family.

The only people listed in the obituary are her deceased mother and her aunt. As the song ended crying could be heard from different directions in the vestibule.

A older but stylish black woman stepped up to the podium and tapped the mic

> *"Hello everyone, my name is Beonca Jennings. I am Briann's auntie. I know to all of you she was the all-powerful head of head of a Cosmetic Empire, but to me she was just little Bri Bri. After my sister passed on to glory, I raised her the best I could and she has always made us proud. So today as I send her to be with my beautiful sister I want you all to know that she was loved." Wiping tears from her eyes she exited the podium and took her seat.*

The remainder of the funeral was a blur, there were more dedications to both Bri and Jason. Startisha stared at the picture of Jason and Bri and thought about herself and Jakari. She would never have a picture like this with Jakari.

Last week she had a private ceremony with just immediate family as they buried Jakari, it still pained her to think that she would never be married to the love of her life, have his babies, and grow old with him. The tears fell uncontrollably from her eye, wetting the obituary. Through watery eyes the face that she saw staring back at her was Bri's.

It was as if Bri was speaking to her, giving her the strength to push forward and that's exactly what she planned to do.

The tears falling on her hands woke her from her daze. She smiled, even after all of the pain she endured over the last year at least the merger between Glamour Girl and Beauty Mark was a success. According to the established by-laws Startisha inherited it all. Bri didn't have any kids or siblings to step forward and Startisha was the next in line in the Duke family. After a failed attempt at a law suit by Momma Duke, Startisha was awarded the company.

She wasn't sure how she felt about finally being recognized as a Duke. It didn't come with the family feeling that she hoped it would.

Instead of letting it all get to her she spent the last six months focusing on growing her company knowledge and taking self -defense and weapons training as a coping mechanism. She knew Lance was still out there somewhere and she never wanted to be vulnerable ever again.

Finishing up another long day, Startisha sat back at her desk with a mixture of emotions. She was tired, yet she didn't want to go to her empty, lonely house. She couldn't bring herself to move out of the house that she shared with Jakari. There were so many memories in her home. Some days, she swore she could still smell him and took comfort in that. All of the employees were gone for the day so the chime of the elevator took her by surprise. Quickly getting up from her desk, Startisha popped the safe she had built into the floor beneath her desk, grabbed her twin Glocks, glasses, and her remote.

She stepped on her special button before she made her move as she talked softly to herself *If anyone other than Publishers Clearinghouse comes through that door with a big ass check, I'm shooting them on sight.* Her heart was pumping fast as hell but she wasn't scared; she was pissed.

Shielding herself in a predetermined spot, she waited. The initial blast shook her entire office, causing Startisha to hold her breath so hard, she threatened to suffocate herself. She could hear men talking.

"Where the fuck did the little bitch go!? She didn't leave the building, or did she slip by you!?" Lance yelled angrily to his partner.

They were searching around her office, kicking over furniture and turning over file cabinets. She recognized her cousin's voice. He was back to kill her but she wasn't having that shit. It wouldn't be long before they found her, so she had to make a move now! Using a remote, Startisha hit a button that made the lights go off.

Next, she pulled her stylish night vision glasses down and took aim. The moment she blasted, the retaliation started. The level of gunfire in the room could cause a small war.

She could see the body of the other guy who came in her house on the floor with blood running from his head. She wanted to jump up and shout *fuck yeah!* Instead, she said a silent prayer to Jakari. A bullet caught her in the shoulder, causing her to drop to one knee. Unfortunately, she had been here before, she was in so much pain.

This time, she was better prepared to handle the situation. Scooting across the room, Startisha fired back, cursing Lance at the same damn time.

Lance was impressed with Startisha. He noticed she had that Duke heart right before he'd shot her the last time. Now he could tell she'd added a deadly aspect to her repertoire; he liked it. Too bad he was going to have to kill her.

While she was focusing on shooting in one area, Lance circled around to the other side undetected. Smiling, he snuck up behind her, placing his gun to her head as he said, "I see you pretty nice with the Glock, but you ain't no killa." Lance pulled her up from her shooting stance by her hair.

The shot that was fired took the entire room by surprise. Nonetheless, Lance's head exploding was just the type of surprise Startisha needed at the moment.

Gazing around the room, she locked eyes with him as she heard him say, "She might not be a killa, but I am." The smoke was still rising from Detective Colston's gun as he pulled a shaking Startisha into his arms. Rubbing her back, he whispered in her ear, "It's over...you are truly the Last Duke Standing."

The end.

I hope you enjoyed Open Marriage. Be sure to check out other work by me. And as always, thank you for your support.

Moon

Catch up on all the criminal romance you can handle from Fanita Moon Pendleton. Available on Kindle at www.amazon.com or www.urbanmoonproductions.com

Coming Soon From Blaque Diamond Publications
Part 2 of the Moet Story

Moet's Revenge

<u>What Happens in Vegas...</u>

Moet didn't set out to be a Boss. She actually had a different plan for her life, but sometimes tragedy molds you into who you really are.

Harry Blake was born into the life. The streets called him Killa, and he was damn good at it. The only soft spot in his heart belonged to one woman. However, knowing what to do with those feelings was a different story.

Follow Moet as she discovers the inner strength to deal with her deep scars and emotions. Through it all, she will learn how to Act Like A *Lady* and Think Like A *Boss.*

About The Author

Born and raised in Oakland, California, Fanita Pendleton relocated to Norfolk, Virginia during her senior year in high school. Since then, she has called the magnificent city home. Fanita began her career as a Juvenile Probation Officer. Later, she worked in Adult Probation before taking a short break to pursue her love of teaching as a Criminal Justice Instructor at a local technical college. Recently, Fanita stepped back into law enforcement and is now a Parole Officer.

Fanita blazed on the scene with her Criminal Romance Series: *Shoot First Ask Questions Never; Fist Full of Tears; Fist Full of Tears: The Sequel; The Moscato Diaries; Act Like A Lady, Think Like A Boss: Vegas*; and *MOET: Money Over Everything*. An avid reader, Fanita holds a special place in her heart for the unsung genre of Urban Crime and Urban Romance Dramas.

In her youth, she devoured the works of literary greats such as Donald Goines and Iceberg Slim. She is an author with SBR Publications and a card-carrying member of The Bankroll Squad #TBRS Family.

Fanita is the owner of Blaque Diamond Publications as well as Urban Moon Productions Company where she is currently providing opportunities to young authors to make their dreams come true.

Fanita received her Master's Degree in Public Administration from Troy University, a Bachelor's in Sociology from Langston University, as well as her Associates in Communications from Luzerne County Community College.

She enjoys shooting pool competitively as well as during her leisure time. Her favorite pastime is catching a football or basketball game with her son, who is the inspiration of her dreams.

Connect with Fanita on *Facebook:* Fanita Moon Pendleton; *Instagram:* #FanitaPendleton; *Twitter*: @Moon081471, or via her website: http://www.urbanmoonproductions.com.

Tales of A Plus Size Diva: Lillian's Story by Shauntrell
Perry

Tales of A Plus Size Diva Part 2 by Shauntrell Perry
Justifiable Insanity by Jauwel
Self Made Bitch by Jauwel
Self Made Bitch 2 by Jauwel
A Daughters Rage by Roni J.
A Daughter's Rage Part 2: Mona's Revenge by Roni J.
Diary of A Hood Princess by K.L. Hall
Diary of A Hood Princess Part 2 by K.L. Hall
Diary of A Hood Princess Part 3 by K.L. Hall
Taste Like Kandi by Keita B
Taste Like Kandi 2 by Keita B
FML: Fuck My Life by Mimi Ray
FML: Fuck My Life Part 2 by Mimi Ray
FML: Fuck My Life Part 3 by Mimi Ray
The Triple Cross: Love Is Not A Game by Mimi Ray
I Am That Bitch by Cinnamon Brown
I Am That Bitch 2 by Cinnamon Brown
I Am That Bitch 3 by Cinnamon Brown
Our Babies Daddy by Cinnamon Brown
Our Babies Daddy 2 by Cinnamon Brown
The Moscato Diaries by Fanita Moon Pendleton
Never Bite The Hand That Feeds You by Cashmeout
Never Bite The Hand That Feeds You Part 2 by
Cashmeout
Act Like A Lady, Think Like A Boss: Vegas by Fanita
Pendleton, K.L. Hall, Shauntrell Perry

Act Like A Lady, Think Like A Boss: Baltimore by Mimi
Ray and Keita B
Act Like A Lady, Think Like A Boss: Miami by Mimi
Ray and Jauwel
Love Don't Love Nobody by Sweet Pea
Love Don't Love Nobody 2: The Seed by Sweet Pea
Chaos: Life As We Know It by Shanard Smith
Loving A Baller by Chantel Sills

Coming Soon from Blaque Diamond Publications and

<u>Urban Moon Productions Company</u>

Tales of a Plus Size Diva Part 3 by Shauntrell Perry
Justifiable Insanity Part 2 by Jauwel
Self Made Bitch Part 3 by Jauwel
Taste Like Kandi Part 3 by Keita B
A Daughter's Rage Part 3 by Roni J.
Loyal 2 a G by Roni J.
Mocha: The Ultimate Sacrifice by Meka
The Triple Cross: Love Is Not A Game 2 by Mimi Ray
Loving A Baller 2 by Chantel Sills
Unbreakable by Keita B
Love Don't Love Nobody 3 by Sweet Pea
Chaos: Life As We Know It Part 2 by Shanard Smith
Moet's Revenge by Fanita Pendleton
Moscato Diaries 2 by Fanita Pendleton

If you have a manuscript you would like us to review and/or want to be placed on the BDP Newsletter list, email us at:

Blaquediamondpublications@gmail.com

Visit our *Facebook* Fan Page at Blaque Diamond Publications.

Open Marriage: A Fatal Attraction Story

Fanita Moon Pendleton

Open Marriage: A Fatal Attraction Story